YARA

A NOVEL

TAMARA FAITH BERGER

COACH HOUSE BOOKS, TORONTO

first edition

Published with the generous assistance of the Canada Council for the Arts and the Ontario Arts Council. Coach House Books also acknowledges the support of the Government of Ontario through the Ontario Book Publishing Tax Credit.

LIBRARY AND ARCHIVES CANADA CATALOGUING IN PUBLICATION

Title: Yara / by Tamara Faith Berger.
Names: Berger, Tamara Faith, author.
Identifiers: Canadiana (print) 2023047117X | Canadiana (ebook) 20230471188 | ISBN 9781552454671 (softcover) | ISBN 9781770567733 (EPUB) | ISBN 9781770567757 (PDF)
Subjects: LCGFT: Novels.
Classification: LCC PS8553.E6743 Y37 2023 | DDC C813/.6—dc23

Yara is available as an ebook: ISBN 978 1 77056 773 3 (EPUB), 978 1 77056 775 7 (PDF)

BIRTHRIGHT

I arrived in your country in August 2006. *Shalom*, the only word I knew in Hebrew.

The night before, I'd been with my girlfriend, arm to arm on a bench, watching fireworks. The floodlit air fogged with barbecue smoke. Speakers hung slanted from telephone poles. There was some kind of street party near where she'd rented us a room.

'I always knew you were going to leave,' said my girlfriend.

My eyes followed the lights that shot up white and disintegrated arterially. She never seemed ten years older than me. I thought, fireworks are broken tubes. Shoelaces running away from the shoes.

A group of men near our bench tried to get us to dance. The hot air made dents in their T-shirt armpits. Families around us ate meat stuck on sticks. Strung street lights left glints on the tops of their heads.

My girlfriend slung her arm around my neck. She loved acting macho. Everyone thought she was a model. I'd talked to my girlfriend about travelling all the time. She knew how much I wanted to see New York and Paris, the islands of Greece.

One guy licked a skewer. He wiggled his hips. My girlfriend plucked me off the bench. Her main action in public was always to ward off the men, and I was supposed to be her sidekick. She said that the stories of my life and of her life had been braided into one.

My mother had ambushed me two weeks ago with the ticket.

Israel was not on my wish list. Israel had never entered my mind.

My mother predicted that I would be tempted.

'Don't go there. Don't take it,' my girlfriend had said.

My girlfriend was going to be thirty years old in a month.

Birthright is a trip that Jewish kids get to go on to Israel. You can be born Jewish anywhere in the world.

I was twenty years old. Never once left Brazil.

My stomach pushed into the band of my jeans as we walked through the lit streets to the room that she'd scored.

I didn't care about our age gap. I always knew about the future.

I always knew that a braid had three strands.

✦

My seatmate had nubs in his ears, hands turned up in his lap. The guy's meal in plastic was sweating, untouched. Short white hairs poked out like fork tines all over his jaw. He laid his pink earplugs like jewels on his tray. Through the window, the clouds looked like paper cut-outs.

'You seem young to be travelling alone,' the man said.

I thought, I've been drinking and fucking since I was fifteen.

The man smiled at my silence. He signalled to the flight attendant walking the aisle. 'Tell her what you'd like.'

'Champagne, please,' I said to the flight attendant's skirt.

Then I placed my hands like his on my lap, palms up. I remembered that the first time me and my girlfriend had sex, it felt like falling backwards into glass.

My mother was mad at what I chose to wear on the plane: this old see-through tank top, fringed jean shorts, and beat-up flip-flops. They'll send you back, she said, trying to get me to change. But I was leaving my girlfriend after almost five years. I was superstitious. She loved my thighs decorated with loose white jean strands.

'So, you have family in Israel?' the man asked.

He had a long, prickly nose with a bump on the bridge. Once upon a time, mine had been exactly like that.

'If you're backpacking,' the man said, 'you must visit Petra, in Jordan. The salt flats. It's a whole hidden city in there.'

A mini-bottle of champagne was placed on my tray. The flight attendant poured half into a plastic wine cup. Her nails were pink and animal-length. The man seemed at least fifty, a mountaineer type: wild hair, meditation, flask of whisky. He lifted his cup to my cup. Our rims didn't fit. I drank my first shot exactly like pop. I liked being in this cabin, our room of two seats.

I thought, all my jean shorts bore orgasm stains.

You will not last a week, my girlfriend prophesied.

'I am going to see my mother,' the man said, rubbing his pant leg. 'She left home; it's been fifteen years. Right after my first daughter was born. She left because she liked it better over there.'

'You have a fifteen-year-old? Wow.'

The man shifted a bit, avoiding his tray. He got his wallet from his back pocket and flipped through it like a book.

'Little Miya,' he said, showing me a photo of a girl with brown skin and pigtails like piano legs.

The clouds in the bubble behind his head flickered pink.

My whole life changed its course at fifteen.

'Me and my brother were born in Netanya,' the man said, shutting his wallet and shifting around his meal tray again. 'My mother said that she wanted us to be settled in our lives – in the New World, she called it – and then she'd go back. We'd lived in Israel only three years.'

A sickening chicken smell filled the airplane.

'So, my father moved back with my mother to Israel. He never wanted to go. He loved football and his friends in Brazil. But my mother kept talking about the flowers, hibiscus, the smell of their tree in the yard. Magenta, the colour. She called it the "perfume of yore." She worked on my father this way for years.'

The man signalled for more whisky, raising his hand. 'But as soon as they got there, the government made them go through the whole thing again, the pledging, the forms, as if they'd never lived there before. They wanted to go back to our old neighbourhood, my mother kept talking about the block, the yard with the tree, *magenta, magenta*, hibiscus everywhere. But when they arrived, they were put in a pen, my father said, a holding pen. My father phoned us, he said they were like goats in the desert being measured for sickness, organ failure, gout. He was laughing, he said they'd been herded like goats, that this wasn't the welcome of which my mother had dreamed … '

The man guzzled his droplets. I accidentally hiccupped. I still tasted our syrupy rum from last night.

'My father had a heart attack the first month they were back.'

The man smiled at the flight attendant when she brought us more drinks. He asked her how she was doing. She rolled her eyes and said, 'Work.' She looked like she could've been on a billboard. Lipstick and strained buttons, the blue pencil skirt.

I thought about Little Miya, her pigtails being pulled.

'I'm not trying to get you drunk,' the man said. 'My wife is religious. She won't touch the stuff.'

When we clicked our glasses together, this time the spheres fit.

I wanted to tell him that I could handle alcohol and being turned on. I had experience with my body that he might not believe.

'You can sleep on my shoulder if you're tired,' the man said.

I hadn't said sorry about his father. I felt twisted up inside. My feelings about leaving were half-good and half-bad. I wouldn't miss saying *sorry, I'm sorry I hurt you* endlessly. On the plane I felt happy and guilty, as if my compassion had died.

The man patted his arm, the alleged pillow. My girlfriend liked to sip rum, let it soak into her tongue. I felt my jean shorts' T-shaped seam in my seat. My girlfriend once told me that I had little ridges in my pussy like teeth. I thought about the flight attendant's tight pencil skirt.

'Who are you meeting in Israel?' the man asked.

'Birthright,' I said.

The man looked confused. I remembered her face last night between my legs. Her tongue hot from the rum, burning from what she wanted to say. The room that she'd rented had walls of owl-eyed wood. My clit pulsed in my jean shorts like a thimble-sized drum. I slithered my hand under the man's meal tray. I took his fist there and turned it upward again.

'Oh?' he said, coughing.

He responded by gripping my wrist.

I smelled alcohol on the hairs of his chin. He held me there, clammy. My cramped pinky, a hook. I wasn't sure what I was doing but I couldn't stop.

'My mother remarried,' the man said hoarsely. 'Last year.'

Maybe, I thought, I should not have touched him first. I remembered her finger, in the thimble, jiggling. Guilt again, happiness, all intertwined.

The man jerked his free hand and waved to the flight attendant again. She arrived at our seats as if she were travelling on ice. When she saw my arm chained, she frowned a little bit before picking up our chicken-breast trays.

I thought, maybe touching people is a mind game.

'Sleepy?' the man whispered. 'Lay your head down.'

The man rearranged all our bottles and lifted the armrest between us.

Suddenly, it was as if a match had been struck. I felt the opposite of sleep. The charged air between us made my chest tight. My breasts felt like crystals prickling through my tank top. When my girlfriend went down on me, it was as if I was hung like a bat.

'I'll tell them you felt sleepy. I'll tell them you're all right.'

His lap was a magnet, I laid my head upside down.

My girlfriend had plush, red-earth lips, always wanting to kiss. My body rushed when we did, a waterfall pummelling my gut. Last night, she was crying. She said I'd get lost in bad dreams. My jean seams were soaked in mid-flight with her lips inside me.

She turned me fluorescent and crackling, a channel of static. Erect.

Mid-blue light from the dome window framed the man's head.

I heard our flight attendant ask if I needed a bag.

'She's fine,' the man whispered. 'She just wanted to sleep.'

My girlfriend predicted that I would not last a week.

You look homeless, my mother said when I'd returned from our motel earlier that day.

Vagina magenta. Hung like a bat.

She'd rimmed the little ridges in my pussy with her tongue.

Now, my mother ordered. We're leaving, Yara. Get your things.

The man raked my skull. The flight attendant reappeared.

'Sir, she can have a whole row to herself.'

I felt heat on my legs. Rung by rung, she went deeper in.

The flight attendant led me to an empty row at the back of the plane.

'I can keep an eye on you here,' she said, smiling at me.

I wanted my own curved pink animal nails. My girlfriend had begged me not to go to Israel. She called it a land of delusion. I thought that was dumb. How could a whole country be deluded? She didn't know what she was talking about. My girlfriend just didn't want me to go anywhere. I stretched out in the three seats at the back of the plane. Needles buzzed in my thighs. I smelled like champagne and pussy. I was glad I wasn't sitting with that man anymore.

I thought, Israel was Israel.

I opened the lid of the blind, eight hours in. My eyes brimmed with a sunrise, violently pink.

The flight attendant brought me my bag from my old seat. Her lipstick was perfect. She winked at me.

The man from Netanya waited for me at the end of the tunnel of arrivals.

'I can take you to Jordan, I can show you the real Israel,' he said.

I spotted a bunch of girls sitting on the ground near a Canadian flag. They all wore oversized white T-shirts with a blue Star of David. A tanned guy with blond hair in a ponytail stalked the circle with a clipboard.

My mother's itinerary told me I was joining a Canadian team.

I told myself I was solid. I walked away from the man. My tongue bore the paste of airplane champagne.

I entered Birthright. I thought, no more mind games.

Before I went under, she looped one fully gloved arm up under my head. She began pinching the tendons alongside my neck.

'When these muscles relax, results are better,' she said.

I didn't know how my neck muscles could lead to my nose. Before she was my girlfriend, she was my nurse.

She found this small, nutlike bump on the slope of my left side and told me to turn my head inward toward her. I smelled her sweat. She dug into me hard. Little mouse sounds from her gloves started to make me feel tense. I told her I was scared of the gas that made me go to sleep.

'I'll be there the whole time. Come, relax into me.'

I heard my exhales on her papery gown as she kept kneading and suctioning me closer to her. Then she clamped down so hard, I felt like it was her teeth. Suddenly, the bump softened; a big flood of heat.

Back then, I thought she was right about surrendering to her pre-surgery.

But this, I realized later, was the birth of my dematerializing.

A girl from the circle of Birthright with a falling-out bun rubbed the slumped spine of a girl in her lap.

'There is no need for worry,' the guy with the clipboard announced. 'Mummy and Daddy have been notified.'

My backpack was lopsided. That slumped girl wept. Hebrew barked out of newscasts on hanging TVs.

'Shalom! You are our Brazilian? Shalom, Brazilian!'

The guy with the clipboard marched toward me, snapping a walkie-talkie into a holster at his waist.

'I'm Aloni,' he said. 'You just missed our news. Twenty rockets from Gaza hit Ashkelon today.'

'Why do they want to kill us?' the slumped girl wailed.

'Brasilia. Ignore her. Welcome to Israel.'

Aloni tossed me a plastic package with a blue-eyed T-shirt and stomped right back over to the crying girl and her friend. 'We do not predict the future,' he said, towering over them.

The slumped girl started to cry even harder.

'Enough!' Aloni yelled. 'You're not in Canada anymore.'

The other kids in the group looked totally dazed, their backpacks all piled by an emergency door. I thought Aloni didn't look that much older than everyone here, but he was acting completely in charge. His flip-flops slapped the floor like cardboard box tops. His face was phosphorescent with tanning oil. Liver-coloured hives bloomed on the neck of the girl who was comforting her friend. I had no idea how close Ashkelon was to here.

Land of delusion. I felt bubbling in my gut.

Aloni dug into an army duffle bag and pitched a few packets of tissues backwards and up through his legs.

'Bull's-eye!' he shouted, trying to make the group laugh.

That girl's hives were like fractals. She opened the packet of tissues, talking to herself. I noticed a spiral-bound notebook on the carpet at her knees. My girlfriend made me promise I'd talk to her from internet cafés.

'We don't send anyone home from Birthright, do you understand? Nothing happens. No one is God here. No one is alone.'

My mother always told me I had a chip on my shoulder. I was at least a year older than these Canadian kids. I hadn't done anything after high school. I stayed all day at my girlfriend's place and read.

I took off my backpack and punctured the plastic-wrapped Birthright shirt. It hung down past my shorts.

'We said we would take care of you. We will take care of you, okay?' Aloni squatted and picked up the crying girl's dirty tissues.

I felt like a prisoner newly released from my cell.

Thank God you're leaving, my mother had said on our way to the airport. That woman was crazy. She would've never left you alone.

Five years and she would not deign to say my girlfriend's name. It was obvious: my mother wanted me to fuck men.

I'd noticed this one guy in the group. He was gangly, with white skin that reflected the light. There were at least fifteen kids here, a lot of them girls. At that point, I didn't think I'd ever be with a woman again.

Aloni herded us all with our packs into a tunnel toward customs.

'In Israel, we prepare ourselves for unwanted situations.'

The airport walls showcased oversized black-and-white photographs. Heavy-lidded men carried boxes uphill in a landscape of rocks.

'Israel is always the scapegoat,' Aloni announced.

I'd never heard that word, *scapegoat*, in English or Portuguese.

A gang of women in sepia army gear smiled and poked their guns into the air. Children's shadowy arms flew out of holes in old trains. We passed by one last black-and-white photograph of three girls in kerchiefs, leaning on half-sunken shovels in the mud.

'If you are in an emergency,' Aloni boomed, 'the best place to be is right here.'

I pictured myself like a goat rooting around the hills of Israel. Almond-shaped nostrils, knobbly horns, wavy spine, and milk teats.

'Hey, hi. You're from Brazil?'

The girl with the hives walked beside me through the tunnel. The blotches on her neck had compacted into buds.

'Reena's freaking about the rockets,' the girl said quietly.

'We will subvert our route up the western coast,' Aloni yelled, walking backwards. 'We will give you all the information as we go.'

'Do we need a gas mask?' some guy asked.

Reena whimpered behind us. 'I want to go home.'

'You are home, this is home,' Aloni said, as he marched up to Reena and shepherded her away.

'What a tool,' the girl said. 'Rescue me. Please.'

The girl was holding the notebook that had been on the ground at her knees. Of course, I knew Israel was supposed to be the home of the Jews.

'I'm Tal. From Toronto. What's your name?'

'Brasilia, over here!' Aloni shouted.

I shrugged at Tal – sorry, the tool's calling me.

I got out my passport that my mother had rushed. My face looked so grim, my lips soldered shut. My girlfriend said I looked like Joan of Arc. I was pretty sure that she hated me now.

I stood in the line behind a group of pilgrims from China.

Tal waved at me from the Canadian-U.S. horde.

She wants to get in your pants. I heard my girlfriend's voice in my head. *You pull people to you because you act so cryptic.*

I didn't need her telling me who I was here.

I watched Tal write in her notebook as she waited in line.

Whenever I wrote anything down on paper, it never sounded like what had just been in my head.

I was not cryptic. I was starting from scratch.

✦

I woke up huffing and queasy that day at the clinic, my neck stuck like a spike in the hospital chair. I called her for the first time six weeks later: alien, unaware. My swelling had gone down. My cough was less wet. She was shocked when I told her how sick I'd been.

I remembered her necklace, a hanging gold cross, lying flat on her papery hospital uniform. She had dyed blond strands in her pulled-back hair. A pecan-coloured forehead and oversized lips. I stared up worm's-eye at the coils of her profile.

'You look pretty,' she said, as soon as I woke.

She handed me a pink plastic hand mirror.

'It takes at least forty-eight hours for the swelling to go down.'

I saw girls being led into the clinic through my stunted peripheral vision.

'If you have any problems,' she said quickly, slipping me her card.

I knew she was doing her job and lying to me. I already understood that plastic surgery reordered society. You were sliced and then let loose to climb up the ladder. It was metamorphosis, sanctioned by the state. And your family was free to psychologically manipulate. My mother told me that her mother had had it done. I knew that was a lie, my grandmother never had the bump. My mother had had me when she was eighteen. She got her nose fixed and said she felt newly attractive to men.

Covered in gauze, I was bulk and blood, broken bridge. When I got home, I didn't want to shower; I refused to brush my teeth. After a week, my mother begged me to get out of bed. Go outside, see your friends, they won't even notice, she said.

But I had this congested, new thing in the middle of my face. Maybe my nose hadn't stopped growing. It felt like a mistake.

After I told my nurse on the phone that I'd been in the hospital, she said, 'Oh God. Thank God. Thank God you called.'

Then she paused for a very long time.

I waited in the kitchen on our phone attached to the wall. There was an air pocket in the wallpaper, the lines didn't sync.

'Why?' I said, into the void.

My nurse from the clinic was model-like. I was sure she had a boyfriend and a partying life. She cleared her throat a few times. Pieces of our wallpaper were not glued down right. Sweat seeped under the receiver and made my cheek wet. Something was wrong. My jaw ached. I was palpably tense.

'Are you still there?'

I knew my mother was insulted that I didn't want a neat nose like hers.

'I would like … ' my nurse started. 'Do you just want to meet up?'

She told me to meet her at Mindu, outside the cafeteria. It had been almost six weeks since my procedure. I'd been face-to-face with her just once. My nurse saw me unconscious. Before the sinusitis.

This almost felt like the beginning of one of my American true crime paperbacks. Teen girl being lured, totally unaware. And the murderer is female, a sexy nurse on the loose. I read true crime books as instructional, how to anticipate murder and rape. That day I met her at Mindu, I was not thinking straight. I forgot my sunglasses. I didn't shave my legs.

It took me thirty minutes to walk there through Novo Aleixo, where you could get liver, intestines, and feet. Blades of fake grass swam in the bloody corners of butchers' displays. Mindu Municipal Park was for tourists, with pink-and-yellow-painted bridges in a maze. When I got there, I pretended I didn't see her walking up to me. Sun sliced my eyes. Children licked soft ice cream. I felt this force field between us. She had bright red lipstick and a bathing-suit-style dress. She really looked like a model, a lingerie one. I saw a little roll of flesh above the line of her underpants. Kids ran around their mothers; their mothers yanked their arms hard. Her hair was wild, all black. There were no more blond streaks. Immediately, I knew that coming here was a mistake.

She stared at my face. 'Are you happy now?' she asked.

My lips stood out more after the nose job. I licked them and folded them in. I thought, true crime was instruction how to not be a dupe.

'You look good. It's all healed. You look sexy,' she said.

She was talking quickly, in spurts. We were the same height, almost the same body type.

'Hey. Looking sexy is a compliment.'

I felt she could be my sister from another life.

She asked if I wanted coffee, if I took sugar or milk.

'Anything,' I mumbled.

It was too hot for coffee, I thought. I watched her walk into the cafeteria, wiry spandex wrinkles around her waist. I started to pace, I regretted saying yes. Cut your nose, plump your ass. You'll fall in love with yourself.

It felt like my tongue was stuck in the ridges of a tube that children's ice cream coils pushed through.

When she emerged from the building, she held out two Styrofoam cups. Her nipples looked like thumbprints. Dead leaves rose from the ground.

She kept looking over at me as we walked down the path.

'Is it okay?' she asked.

I nodded and scalded my tongue. The plastic top leaked a pustule of foam.

We approached an armless green bench in front of a crooked rubber tree.

'Here,' she said.

I put my drink down, twisting to sit.

'You have a bit on your nose,' she said, inching closer, reaching out.

Before she could touch it, I swatted the air.

'Are you okay with us meeting?'

I nodded. My face had been replaced.

'Look, I'm just going to say it … Since you came to the clinic, I can't stop thinking about you.'

I swallowed more foam. I thought I was going to throw up. I knew that she was older than twenty years old.

'Fuck,' she said. 'Look, do you want to hang out with me?'

I was formless and mute like the armless bench we sat on.

'Does that mean yes?'

I nodded my head, completely struck dumb.

✦

After my nose job, to make me feel better, my mother had said, Yara, get ready, boys are going to be crawling to you. I thought about boys on their hands and their knees looking up at my profile – the exact same way I'd seen hers when I was in the chair. I thought about slapping the boys, how I'd seen people do to their pets. I'd tower over them and big-toe their heads to the ground. I hoped that my mother was right. I'd never had a boyfriend. Men flocked to her bedroom; I heard her moaning most nights. But ever since going to Mindu to meet my nurse, I'd stopped telling myself stories about boys all doglike. My mouth was this plump, glossy blossom. My nose neat, aquiline. I saw things happen in a succession of images – like a fashion shoot. Her swinging gold cross. Her black and blond stripes. Nipples through spandex. My mouth on thumbprints.

She was *fuckable*, I knew guys in my class would've said.

But the more days that passed since our first coffee on the bench, the more the whole thing seemed so far-fetched.

Like, why did she say she was thinking about me? Didn't she know my real age? I felt my nose itch. I felt sure she stroked every girl's arm as they went under. I felt sure that she greeted every single one with that same plastic mirror when they woke. I couldn't function at school. I could barely even eat. I drank milk with a straw. I could tolerate soft ice cream. Questions got parsed in my head. What did her thinking about me actually mean? And how did looking sexy fit in?

I decided to put on lipstick for our second time. I wore a crop top and jean shorts. I wanted something.

She'd arrived before me at Mindu on our bench. She was sitting there smoking with crossed legs in flip-flops. Her slick black hot pants like a braided horse tail.

God, what could I ever say to this person that wouldn't make me sound dumb?

'Do you think I'm old?'

That was the first thing she said when I sat down. Tree roots twisted in front of us, knobbly and pronged.

'No,' I said, squeezing my thighs together till they hurt.

'Well, I feel like I'm old. And I feel like you think I'm old, too.'

Before I could say no again, she told me that she'd been working at the clinic for three years. She had a cosmetic assistant's certificate and she wanted to go to nursing school.

'You think that's a good idea?' she asked, blowing smoke away from me. 'I was a real fuck-up in high school. I don't know if I could pass.'

My lips stuck together from the lipstick. At fifteen, I didn't know it was a Jewish thing. I mean, being good at school and shrinking your beak.

'I need a better job,' she said. 'So I can spin. I love house. You like house? All my friends are DJs.'

The clouds were a graph made of pillows overhead. I wondered which high school she'd gone to. And what did *fuck-up* mean?

'I bet you're really good at school.'

It was like she could read my mind. I felt myself trying not to smile. I liked studying English and reading true crime. I'd just read *Helter Skelter* and I couldn't stop thinking about that actress, Sharon Tate.

'I dropped out,' she said. 'Wasn't meant for book shit.'

I was trying not to think about how different I already knew that we were. I tried to focus on just saying something simple back to her. But I felt far away, blank, like one of those Charles Manson girls. Doe-eyed, hypnotized, thrumming everywhere.

She sighed and stood up. I knew she wanted me to speak. I actually wanted to say *yes* and just be right here. Her white tank top billowed, her hot pants reflected the sun. It occurred to me that this whole time I'd assumed she was a nurse.

'I'm trying to quit,' she said after a few puffs of a fresh cigarette.

I stared at her red shellacked toes and junkyard cigarette butts. I hadn't told my mother where I was or when I'd be home.

I dreamed of being an adult, escaping our house. My mother was teaching me how to clean chicken, how to separate eggs. You need to learn how to function when I'm not here, she said. We lived alone in our Adrianópolis high-rise. It was always just us. I think my mother thought that she was preparing me for the 'real world.'

'Look, I'm just going to say it.'

Her eyes were glassy, laser-like.

'I think, maybe, Yara … I'm in love with you.'

The tubes of my nose burned. I glared at the dry, broken ground.

'I have to go now,' I said.

I felt bile rise. Dead leaves were burned here, I thought, to make mulch. I tried to stand up. She took a step toward me.

'Wait,' she said. 'Wait.'

But I started to run. The sky was white and electric. There was no 'real world.'

I ran up the pathway back to the cafeteria. I was sweating, so stupid. How could a woman be in love with me? I'd thought I loved this guy once when I was thirteen. I felt sick. I felt dread. That was nothing like this. My flip-flops slapped the ground. Thinking about being in love was not the same as feeling it.

✦

Tal wrote in her notebook with her marbled green gel pen. Through the crack in the seats from behind on the bus, I spied the words *mother* and *Israel*.

On all the highway billboards, a bone-grey, teenaged soldier with glasses leaned up against a wall. His khaki shirt was unbuttoned. He looked emaciated. Everything in Israel so far seemed so strange. Emergencies, weeping, Frankenstein-looking men.

The guy I noticed from the airport poked my shoulder from behind.

'Check it out,' he said, slipping me his phone through the gap.

His phone had a little typewriter with an oblong screen on top. I'd never seen one like this; people at home had flip-style.

I didn't know that a phone could show a video like TV. I turned around and stared at the guy through the gap in our seats. He was pitched forward, too close to my face. His breath was swampy, like herbs left in water too long.

'Turn up the sound.'

'Dude, just let her watch,' the guy beside him said.

I looked at the phone. I heard a low drone. I saw bobbing black spheres, little dots pixillated. I realized those were heads. I realized the video was bird's-eye, a crowd of people moving forward, some kind of parade. Buildings leaned around them, decorated with red-and-green flags.

'My name's Jonah,' the guy said, pushing his nose through the crack.

He stared at my thighs smashed on the carpeted bus seat.

'It's revenge for Gilad,' the guy beside Jonah said.

'You know, the soldier who was just abducted,' Jonah added. 'That's why rockets are flying up north.'

I heard the other guy laugh. 'What, has she been living under a rock?'

Suddenly, Tal scooted into the empty seat beside me. 'Don't listen to Joel. He's full of shit. Everyone's talking about the soldier who was abducted: Gilad Shalit.'

'Keep watching,' Jonah said.

Joel hissed, 'Revenge is a bitch.'

'It might spark a new intifada,' Jonah said.

'Why do you love saying that word, bro?'

'Oh my God, bitch fight. They go like tomcats,' Tal said.

I'd heard of the word *intifada*, but I wasn't sure exactly what it meant. We kept looking at the phone. The men's chanting grew really loud. The walls of the buildings had tar-coloured gouge marks.

'Hamas dragged Gilad through a tunnel to Gaza,' Jonah said.

'Israel will incinerate the perpetrators,' Joel added, under his breath.

'My mother almost didn't let me come here because of this,' Tal said.

'Tell your mother she needs to worry more about Lebanon,' Joel spat.

'Fuck off. Oh my God. Yara, don't listen to them.'

I thought, what happened in this country didn't affect me like it did them.

Gaza is an open-air prison, my girlfriend had said.

A pixellated, rocket-shaped box came into view on Jonah's phone. It was sliding forward on top of the men. That was a casket. There was a dead man inside. His head was half-wrapped in a black-and-white scarf. I knew those scarves, they sold them at the market near my girlfriend's place. They meant revolution. The coffin kept veering. The body tipped side to side, like a leaf in a creek. Then another coffin came forward: three caskets floating downstream. People crammed together. We watched bird's-eye. Then the face of one man – sunken, bloodless – suddenly zeroed in unexplained on Jonah's screen.

'Fuck, this is intense,' Tal whispered, bouncing her legs.

I didn't want to watch this. I turned my head away.

I was in Israel because my mother wanted me here. I was in Israel to escape my girlfriend.

Israel is always the *scapegoat*, Aloni had said.

'Brasilia,' whispered Jonah. 'Is that your real name?'

I was spooked. What was *scapegoat*? What did it mean?

'Have you even heard her speak yet?'

Tal reached under my hand to help steady the phone.

I remembered our armless green bench – mine and my girlfriend's. *Scapegoat*. Throat closing. How much I hadn't said.

'What? You kids never seen a dead body before?'

Aloni was there, suddenly blocking our aisle.

I tried to turn down the volume on the phone but I didn't know how. Tal took away her hand. Gaza played on. I shoved the phone on the seat between my legs. Reading about dead people was different than seeing it.

'When I was doing army service five years ago,' Aloni said, 'a terrorist tried to blow us up. This was 2001, you remember, right after the attacks.'

Aloni shifted the bags he was carrying into one fist. He pitched his tanned, oily face right over top of me and Tal.

'He thought we weren't expecting him, but we were prepared. These people think Israel did 9/11, do you understand? Now they kidnap our soldiers and try to infiltrate our won land.'

I covered the still-buzzing phone between my legs with both palms. Aloni dropped a wax-wrapped piece of bread down into Tal's lap.

'Gilad is alive,' Aloni said. 'But if they keep him from us, they will have more men to put in the ground. Israel, you should understand, does not play around.'

Aloni left us and walked backwards, distributing bread to the rest of the bus. The air conditioning blew into my skull. I hadn't thought about 9/11 in a long time. Tal chewed her lips. I was putting things together as much as I could. Gilad Shalit on the billboards, caskets, and intifada …

'See? The Arabs want to kill us,' Joel whispered through the crack from behind. 'We should pour concrete over them. All the way to the sea.'

'Fuck you and your mother,' Tal said, mashing the bread between her hands.

I gave the phone back to Jonah. I thought, Israeli true crime.

I remembered when I got home from school that day in 2001, my girlfriend had called and hung up ten times on our machine. When I called back, she'd yelled, Where the fuck have you been? She knew I was at school. I was in secondary then. By the time I'd walked to her place, I saw what had happened in New York. All the TVs were on in the bars, every single screen showing exactly the same thing. Freak black explosions. Fibreglass human beings. I stood beside men watching those planes disappear again and again. It was hard to walk forward. I tried to hug my girl-friend at her door.

'How did they not fucking tell you all day?' She let out a sob.

Those planes flew into the buildings at her place, too. Her TV was tiny with a circular antenna on top. She thought that our teachers should've let us go home. My girlfriend hated America. She kept asking me how many people I thought were running down the stairwells inside. Her living room smelled like rubbing alcohol. She said that TV was mind control. The planes kept nosing the towers. Then the towers fell in. I thought about my mother and grandmother watching this on repeat. Bodies like flies. Buildings as animation. My girlfriend said this was a sign of the end of the world. Tactics of overstimulation, tactics of propaganda. America raped Guatemala. America burned Vietnam. I'd known her for only four months in September 2001. She always swore that she'd never step foot on that land.

I heard Joel chewing behind me, his mouth making yeast. Jonah's phone was still on, sirens and Hebrew.

'Do you know what's happening?' I said to Tal, wanting only her to hear.

'Stuff like this always happens in Israel. They'll send us home if it gets bad.'

A man's leaflike body zigzagged inside my mind. Tal unwrapped the sticky napkin from the bread in her lap. I saw small roadside shops where men drank tea at tables low to the ground. Ever since I was a kid, I liked reading gruesome, cruel things. Like *Lord of the Flies* and *Watership Down*. I remembered one little rabbit talking about a field full of blood. My grandmother always made fun of me. I was the Grim Reaper, she said.

You shouldn't put things in your head, Yara, that you can't get out.

I loved to sit beside her on her plastic-covered couch and stick my bare arm like tape onto hers. We looked at her gold-tipped family photographs glued into leather albums. I loved this one black-and-white girl with chin-length ringlets who seemed too big to be sitting on her mom's lap.

'That one is Liza, my auntie's daughter,' my grandmother explained, every single time quickly flipping the page.

'Hitler killed Liza. Hitler killed them all.'

Watership Down kept me up all night. Something terrible is going to happen here, the rabbit warned after his bloody vision.

My girlfriend told me that Israelis had been seen celebrating 9/11.

Look, I know you're Jewish, she'd said. But those people are sick in the head.

'Just try and forget it,' Tal said, ripping me a piece of Aloni's bread.

In *Helter Skelter*, Sharon Tate had been stabbed. She was nine months pregnant and her baby was alive.

The bread tasted like mush. Goosebumps graphed my arms.

Outside, rows of squat white houses with red rooftops were embedded in the hills. I imagined blood, thick like paint, barrelling down those slopes.

I thought, me and my girlfriend had watched a massacre just like everyone else.

On the bus, in a sweat, I realized that I spited my girlfriend by fleeing and not telling her why. It occurred to me I'd wasted five years of my life by not thinking for myself.

In Israel, I could finally hear my own thoughts. I could feel how they formed. They rose out of the murk of my mind like mudfish. I could almost see them now, spot-lit, on a platform.

✦

After our second time at Mindu Park, I kept replaying what could've happened in my head. I mean, what would've happened if I hadn't run away. I kept seeing her red toes and cigarette-suckling lips. I needed to know what would happen. I promised myself that this time I would not flee.

I called her this time. I made the date. I wore a bright pink baby-T crop top. I wore my jean shorts again.

When I got to the bench near the river in the park, the first thing I noticed was that her eye makeup was smudged. She told me that she was hungover because she'd been up dancing all night. Her cigarette smoke like a halo. Her wild black hair pulled back in a bun. I thought she actually didn't look that much older than me then. But she sat strangely far from me on our armless green bench.

She said, 'Look, I'm sorry for what happened last time.'

It was like she'd preplanned that sentence. She pitched her cigarette onto the ground.

'I didn't mean anything by it. Can we just forget it. Be friends?'

I felt rocks in my eye sockets. My nostrils compressed.

'C'mon, I'm sorry. Say something. I fucked up, okay?'

What does love feel like with a woman was what I wanted to know.

'Why are we here? This is crazy, Yara.'

I wanted her to light another cigarette. To stay longer with me. But I just sat there when she stood up, crushing my hands. She started walking away and I hated myself. I wanted to shoot an arrow into her jiggling horse tail.

'Don't,' I said, into myself.

She stopped. I stood up. I could feel the leaves breathe.

I felt a weird swell where my real nose had been.

'Look at me when you speak. Yara, please.'

Her harsh, lowered voice raked the seams of my jeans.

I wore this pink crop top on purpose. We stood so apart. The spear-shaped leaves of the rubber tree beat in the wind. I couldn't lift my head. I couldn't look at her eyes. My feet seemed deformed, like cut tentacles, not a part of this land.

'Look, you weren't into it, you weren't into me,' she said.

I wanted to correct her but my tongue was cauterized.

I didn't know it was possible to feel this upset. I wanted to mash my forehead at her feet.

'It's okay,' she said, walking toward me, closing our gap. 'I never expected anything from you. Nothing, okay?'

I swallowed sludge in my throat. I didn't know what was happening to me.

'Please,' she repeated.

I heard her licking her lips.

When I finally looked up, tears were slick on her cheeks. When did she start crying? I was wet in my jeans.

She took one final step toward me. She reached for my forearm. The wind blew through us both. I felt see-through and alone. All of a sudden, her face was at mine and she pushed into me. Like a slimy plant stem, my nose touched her neck. She wiggled a lot. I didn't know why. I felt my bare stomach making circles on hers. We were going to kiss. I felt my vagina on fire. I bit into her neck before it happened. She yelped really loud. Pebbles from the river dragged through my underpants.

'You made me bleed. Look.'

Her first two fingers were pressed on the side of her neck. When she lifted them up, the spot was marked with my teeth. I was going to say sorry, but then she stuck her fingers in her mouth. She licked herself, smiling. I felt amphibian.

She took me by my elbow and led us out of the park a different way than I'd come. The sun made me squint. The cicadas screamed.

Novo Aleixo was one of the neighbourhoods I was allowed to go to with my friends. I'd gone to a café around here where they served gelato. I was looking for that café. Maybe it had closed. We cut through an alley to an area where concrete pink homes lined the road. My knees cracked like a marionette's. I tracked the number of iron gates so I could find my way out. We walked up to an apartment building still under construction. The whole top floor was just walls with copper-coloured spokes pointing out.

We walked up three flights of stairs, out of the sun. I had this feeling she'd found me, a kid lost in the park. There was a lump in my shorts. I thought, maybe I'm growing a dick like some boy. She's going to give me a glass of cold milk and let me call my mom.

✦

We reached Tiberias as the sun was going down. The bus parked at some kind of market near the water. Prayer flags, like kite tails, hung between stalls. Aloni herded us off the bus with our backpacks, making us stay in single file as we headed into the market. Crates in grids filled with nuts sloped beside wrinkled, dried fruits.

'Falafel,' Aloni announced. 'Our national dish!'

Aloni stopped us at a food stand in the corner lit with hanging bare bulbs. There was a rainbow buffet of glass bowls in tiers under the lights.

'Brasilia, have you ever had this wondrous little burger cooked with chickpea?'

I was given a pita, the same bread we had on the bus. This one was hot, wrapped with a wax bow. I stood in a line behind Tal and Reena, stuffing pink pickles from the bowls into my pita with cubed cucumbers and fluorescent hot sauce.

'Very good,' Aloni said, looking at me.

At the end of the line, we handed our pitas to a cook who spooned two balls into it, folding the wax paper over the top. Then we walked back out of the market to a patio across the street. The patio had tables you stood at by desiccated palm trees.

Aloni moved between us all with his clipboard like a hostess.

'You see the date trees, Brasilia? This kind is only in Israel.'

My falafel was saturated and noduled, with a caramel coat. Wind tried to lift up the yellowed, limp leaves of the trees. I wanted to prove to my mother that I was capable of normality. I mean, having friends, travelling, being like Canadians.

I asked Tal, 'Can you take a picture of me?'

I thought of my grandmother's photographs, four or six to a page, with fancy gold corners that held them in place.

Tal had one of the biggest cameras I'd ever seen.

'Director-to-be,' Reena said, sounding proud.

Her camera was the shape of a little dog's head.

'Should I keep eating?' I asked her.

'No. You should stop.'

We went to the little stone wall at the far edge of the patio. The sun had dropped in the sky. I stared at the brackish water far off.

'Like that,' Tal said.

I saw Aloni watching us. This was the Sea of Galilee, that Jesus walked on.

'Don't move your head, Yara. Now, just your eyes.'

I kept hearing the monotone slice of her lens.

'Look here,' Tal said. 'God, you'd be an amazing actress.'

The faraway hills smudged into the sky.

'I mean, you totally have the face.'

I thought, Jesus walked on this water with floppy, callused feet.

'I'm serious, Yara. Have you ever thought about acting?'

Yeah, my girlfriend and my mother had thought about it for me.

'Time to go, Taglit!'

I wondered what Tal would think if I told her I'd been in front of a camera for years. The bump of my nose had been smashed and rebuilt.

I wrapped up my falafel and shoved it in my carry-on.

Aloni called us Taglit, which he said meant *discovery* in Hebrew. He took attendance outside the hostel, a speckled white two-storey building that looked like a saloon. In Israel, he said, Jews discover themselves.

The wind smelled like deep-fry. The sun was a boil.

I remembered how me and my girlfriend used to sit in front of the computer for hours, looking at Myspace, down-loading tracks. Myspace was foreplay for watching other things. My girlfriend liked Britt from FreeCams, who stroked her wrinkled bikini bottoms as she slid on the bed like a snake. Sometimes Britt froze while her fingers were cloaked. When she rejigged, she was in a totally new place on the bed.

What did it mean to discover yourself as a Jew? And why did I think about the camgirls right then, too? It felt like some thought that was broken, halves of the same worm. Saggy plastic vines twisted around the hostel's front desk. There was a circular wooden light fixture and tourist posters for the Dead Sea. A mini-fridge with a piggy bank where Aloni said we could pay for drinks.

'You put your shekels in the box. We trust you and you trust us.'

There was a computer in the corner in a kind of confessional stand.

Tal bought six beers. We brought them up to our room.

My girlfriend always said she thought Britt could be a real model.

'Fuck me. No fridge. We'll have to hoover these,' Tal said.

'I can't drink with my meds,' Reena complained.

'That's okay. Me and Brasilia will get drunk.'

'That's not her real name.' Reena rolled her eyes.

Our room had thick purple bedspreads embroidered with camels, or dogs. My grandmother told me that Jesus was Jewish but He didn't suffer for us.

'*Brasilia* reminds me of *Brazzers*,' Tal said, as she unwrapped her leftover falafel, the foil all pink.

'Gross! C'mon, Tal, tell her what that is.'

'Newfangled Canadian porn,' Tal said, smiling at me.

My falafel had leaked all over the snack-sized nuts from the plane.

'Why don't you just tell us your real name?' Reena whined.

'Yara,' I said, looking for the trash can.

'Yara,' Tal said, following me with her eyes. 'I know everyone on this fucking trip.'

'It's true. Me and Tal have been friends since we were three!'

Tal rolled her eyes at Reena. I liked the way she said my name. She leaned against a cluster of damp-looking pillows, her feet up on the camel's blurred head. *Newfangled Canadian porn*. I couldn't find the trash can.

'What are you writing?' I asked, nodding at her spiral-bound notebook.

'A screenplay,' Tal yawned.

'Tal goes to film school,' Reena said. 'Best program in all of Canada.'

'What's it about?' I asked.

'God, I hate that question.'

'Why?'

'Because I can't just sum up the whole story in one sentence like that.'

'Tal's an amazing writer. She's so talented,' Reena gushed.

Then shouldn't she be able to say what she's writing about? I thought.

Rolling her eyes, Tal got up for another beer. Reena went to the bathroom. I started eating my leftover falafel too fast. Sauce dripped on my bedspread. Gas formed in my gut.

'Is your screenplay a porno or something?'

Tal laughed so abruptly that beer came out of her nose.

'Oh my God, Yara,' she said, coughing. 'Why do you think that?'

Because *Brazzers, Brasilia*. It felt like an invitation.

Tal couldn't stop coughing and laughing. I watched her wipe her face. I wasn't a writer but I felt like proving something.

'On my sixteenth birthday,' I said, really slowly, 'my girlfriend got her friend to tape us having sex. And that's my story. One sentence. Just like that.'

Tal immediately stopped coughing. I thought it felt sort of good to use her own words against her. Then Reena emerged from the bathroom. Face cream stuck like curds in the half rings around her nose.

'What's wrong? Oh my God, Tal. You're totally red.'

I thought, I just pitched my *newfangled* story. I pitched it like a film.

I got up and walked around Reena to get another beer.

Tal covered half her face with the neck of her shirt.

I realized I hadn't thought about that tape in a while. I'd only ever seen it once, and only one part. I remembered how I hated Manny, her best friend, for filming how far my neck stretched. I thought of dead bodies, loose necks, zigzagging downstream.

'What is a *scapegoat*?' I asked Reena on my way back to the bed.

'Oh my God, Yara. Why are you asking that right now?'

'Because Aloni said it at the airport. He said that Israel was one.'

Reena's eyes bulged. She sat beside Tal on the bed. '*Scapegoat*'s when you're blamed for, like, political things, right, Tal?'

'In a sentence: Gilad Shalit is a *scapegoat* for the crimes of Israel.'

'Tal, oh my God. That's not true,' Reena squealed.

I walked away from them to the window. We faced a lit-up parking lot. The parked cars looked like turtles. My girlfriend was jealous, I thought. She was jealous that I was in Israel and living my life. My girlfriend used to say that she could watch me on repeat. She said that Britt, her favourite camgirl, made fifteen hundred U.S. dollars a month. My girlfriend said I looked like a model. She said I'd make more.

'Is *scapegoat* always political?' I asked. 'I mean, is there always a crime?'

But when I turned around, Tal wasn't there and Reena was under the covers, pretending to be asleep.

It occurred to me that maybe the story of me and my girlfriend only made sense in a sixteen-year-old's brain. It occurred to me that maybe I was the scapegoat, always ready to be blamed. Blamed by my girlfriend for not feeling what she felt. The beer neck was slippery, lukewarm in my palm. I knew I didn't look like a model, even with a straight nose. I felt like moving that green pen off Tal's notebook. I walked toward the nightstand and I picked it up. The pen rolled to the carpet. Tal had loopy, slanted script. My mother told me I could still go to college even though it was a year late. She said my grandmother would pay.

I read one sentence in her notebook: *Is Israel my home?*

Then Tal emerged from the bathroom wearing pleated green shorts and a matching sports bra. I crouched down and picked up her pen.

'Reena always falls asleep first. Ever since we were kids. At sleepovers, or wherever, she literally turns off like a switch.'

Tal lay on their bed sideways. I spread out on my back. Air beat on my scalp from the ragged ceiling fan.

'What are you thinking about?' Tal whispered.

'Nothing,' I said.

Then she turned off the gouged lamp between our beds.

'I didn't mean to insult you about the porno,' I said after a bit.

'Oh my God, don't worry. You didn't at all.'

Tal's nose seemed exaggerated in shadows. The sheets were bleached, full of starch. I wondered if her mother ever asked her if she wanted a nose job. I thought, *scapegoat* was a girl, not a country. A scruffy, horned thing you spat on for release.

I didn't want to keep things inside me anymore.

'I wish I knew how to write,' I said out loud.

'Anyone can learn,' Tal said. 'It's not that hard.'

'But on paper it never looks like what was inside my head.'

'It's not supposed to be transcription – that is its trick.'

Like a trap door? I thought. Or like words lost and found?

'I need to ask you something, Yara.'

I nodded in the dark.

'Sixteen-year-olds in a sex tape is kind of dangerous, right?'

'My girlfriend was twenty-five when we met.'

Tal bolted up and turned on the wrecked, bulbous light. 'Um, you know that's illegal?'

My sandpaper tongue flattened out like a crepe.

'Yara, what you're telling me is statutory rape.'

Tal pitched forward, animated, into the space between our beds. 'You have the evidence, don't you? You have a sex tape? There's a five-year statute of limitation for filing charges of sexual exploitation.'

I was confused.

'The legal age for sex in Brazil is fourteen,' I said.

'Not with an adult, Yara, oh my God.'

'Shhhhhh,' Reena hissed. 'I'm trying to sleep.'

Heat from the light bulb sizzled on my front teeth. Tal's face looked distorted. I had no idea where that tape was, or if Usenet existed at all anymore.

'My father is a lawyer, Yara. I know about these things.'

I started doing pressured calculations in my head. I got my nose fixed in March 2001. Then, after two weeks, I got really sick. I had to be pumped full of drugs. My mother rushed me to the hospital. It was sinusitis. Concrete cracks in the bridge of my nose. I remember my mother's face blurred at my bedside. She looked like an egg. She begged me to speak, but I didn't know where to speak from. I remember my throat was plugged up. My saliva, egg whites. All I could feel were these gluey beige yawns.

'Say something,' Tal whispered.

My voice slithered out. 'You want to charge my girlfriend on her thirtieth birthday?'

'Yes. She's a sex offender. You can't fuck someone underage.'

I thought, the crime of the scapegoat is the sex tape. I always told myself I'd called my girlfriend that first time out of boredom. In the hostel with Tal, it occurred to me that that wasn't the case. I'd called my girlfriend the first time because she'd seen me when I was under. She'd seen me when I was being altered. Unicorned.

'Yara, I want to know what happened to you.'

I remembered running away that first night from her place. Running down that dirt hill past the dogs behind gates. I remembered that when I got home, I vomited, missing the bowl. My mother was freaked out. She thought it was the infection coming back.

'I threw up after the first time it happened,' I said, hoarse.

'Because you knew deep down that it was wrong,' Tal said.

'No.'

'I mean, your body knew. Your body knew what was wrong.'

I felt my girlfriend through the ocean, begging me to throw her a line.

My mother had wanted to take me back to the hospital that night. I remember thinking that my girlfriend's fingers inside me had opened a new channel inside.

'My mother is a survivor of sexual abuse,' Tal said.

I felt like my tongue was the root of my nose. As if my nose was a horn, my tongue wasn't properly stuck. I remembered the way that my girlfriend's tongue grew. I was breathing too fast, like I was slipping downhill. Tongues were oversized slugs. Her tongue made me come. She tied the ribbon round the horn. Nozzle breathing, my girlfriend, I couldn't hold on.

'Have you ever wanted to come to Canada?' Tal asked.

'My mother is way better at articulating these things.'

I didn't want to meet her mother. Or her father, either. I didn't want to talk about this ever again. All I wanted was to fall backwards, free-fall, hold on to nothing. I had a longing for pestles, her lava-like cunt. The first time I'd licked her, I remembered, she had already licked me ten times. The first time I tried it, she lay there and spread her thighs wide. *Throw me a line. Come on, throw me a line.* My girlfriend had hairs curled around her cunt like a bat. I nuzzled and stuck my tongue in way too fast. The heat was a shock. I felt this poisonous flush. It was like nosing a bump in the underbrush. There at her legs, I felt a liver-coloured egg. I poked it to pierce it. I lapped the great gush.

Tal said it was illegal. She said statutory rape.

My girlfriend said I could have it again any time.

✦

A cat jumped off the coffee table as we walked in. Records lay around dusty, all out of their sleeves.

'Sorry for the mess,' she said. 'That's not my cat.'

She shooed it out of the room and into the kitchen.

Accordion blinds covered an oblong window. I had to clear dirty plates to give myself space on the couch. Water gurgled through the ceiling. A lump grew in my throat. Where had she just gone? And where did she sleep?

I stared at a burnt beeswax candle on the floor. Behind the candle was a black-and-white photograph of a man and woman on their wedding day. A white sheet was caked with the dust of incense. I imagined that those were her grandparents.

She came back into the room in a long white T-shirt. Her shins were shiny, I noticed, like she'd just moisturized.

'I should call my mother,' I whispered, staring at the woman's veil in the photograph. No eyes. Just nostrils. A lace collar up to her chin.

I remembered her nipples through the fabric. That purplish bite mark on her neck. I felt like I was going to pass out when she sat in front of me, barefoot. I mean, I was on the couch and she was curled up on the floor.

'I really didn't know that you felt anything,' she said.

The telephone dematerialized. So did my mom.

I was clenching my jaw. She laid her iron cheek on my knee.

'You smell so good,' she said.

I thought I was going to die.

'It's okay,' she said, looking up, licking her bottom lip.

My guts felt all twisted, like hot dog balloons.

I watched as she let her tongue touch my kneecap.

God, what was she doing? It felt like fire through bone.

I knew I used to look one way in the mirror and now I looked different. I blamed my mother for this problem, this slip in my face. I had a new nose and a new circumstance.

She giggled. 'Come on, just think of me as your cat.'

But I didn't know cats. We'd never had pets. My nose was my mother's gift to me, pre–Sweet Sixteen.

'Wait,' I squeaked.

I think I was anticipating pain. It was as if someone had opened a vault and pushed me inside.

'Are you okay?' she asked, suddenly perched on the couch beside me like that cat.

I felt like my knee had been shaved and shellacked.

She started stroking my arm, like she'd touched me in the surgeon's chair.

'Do you think I'm too old for you, is that it?'

I wished she'd stop talking about age.

'Let's stop then. If you think so, let's stop right now.'

She shuffled away from me, making me cold. I really didn't care how old she was. Like, I knew she was an adult. I knew she had a job. I thought things would be okay if we could just talk like friends. But I didn't know what to say or how to make things more straight. She lit a cigarette. She wasn't looking at me then. I started to shiver. I really didn't want her to be mad. I just stared at the photo of her grandparents on the floor. The man in the photo had stony, far-apart eyes.

'I pray when I need things,' she said, looking at him, too.

I felt a cold liquid rush through my gut as if I was going to shit. The flesh of my bum spread into a gelatinous pulse. It almost felt like she was doing this, touching me with her mind. I really, really wanted her closer again.

'I'm cold,' I whispered.

She looked right at me. I think she thought I was lying. I finally looked back at her.

'I'm sorry,' I whispered.

'Don't be sorry. For what?'

'For running away.'

'It's okay,' she said, with a strange little shrug.

Then her hand touched my elbow, right where I'd wanted it. Her fingers tickled up my inner arm toward my shoulder. I felt like I was going to laugh.

'Is this okay?' she asked.

I nodded. I kept my mouth closed. I couldn't breathe deeply. I wanted her to touch me exactly like this.

'I've never felt this way about someone before,' she said quietly.

Then she slid herself even closer to me than she'd been before. She closed her eyes and I watched as her fingers slid up my neck to my lips. I heard myself squeak. She touched the tip of my nose. My insides buzzed loud, like bees. She pushed her fingertip into my mouth. Then she opened her eyes and slid her finger in.

'Yara, you're so sweet.'

I couldn't breathe right. I opened my mouth to take her all in. I wanted to be sexy, not sweet, as I sucked her fingertip. It tasted like candy. She circled inside. Me and my mother had looked at so many photos of actresses, how a woman's nose sat in the middle of her face.

'Close your eyes, it's okay,' she said.

Her curved-up eyelashes, her caramel-coloured eyelids. My grandmother had told me, You can be Jewish anywhere in the world. I let myself sleep as her finger slid in and out of my mouth. It was jointed, now salty. She kept slipping it deeper each time. I heard myself hum. Saliva came forth in waves. I smelled her sweat, I knew it, a bunched-up handker-chief. She fingered my mouth like the needle of a sewing machine.

Sweet and salty together. Salty and sweet. My mother made me choose the nose of my favourite actress. My mother wanted me to have a 'European nose.' My mother said she wanted me to have options in the world.

My mouth filled with froth. My mouth felt like a ship. She finally slid out her finger. I felt like an actress.

I felt an aura, a steam of Jewishness.

I felt like I could be the messenger of sex.

There was no break in what happened between me and her. I mean, after her finger, she put her lips onto mine. We were suddenly kissing. It was completely full on. I tasted myself as her tongue pushed in again and again. Her mouth was better than her finger. My mother showed the surgeon a picture of Sonia Braga as a teen. I felt underwater sound waves ripple through my skull. I tasted like sea foam. I sucked on her lips.

'Yara, I didn't know how much you wanted this.'

I thought, kissing is like drowning with your nose sticking out.

I reached out for her thigh. It was slick as seaweed. She climbed on my lap. The cat wanted to be touched. I couldn't believe how she kept pumping her tongue in and out of me. She felt satiny, feline, totally gigantic. Her hands pulled the edge of my crop top. My vagina multiplied. I imagined the white rim of fat that's on steak. She wiggled on my lap. She gave me her full weight. I didn't know how this would end. I had a math test the next day. Her tongue was so much bigger than her finger. I tried to hold on. She kept wiggling around. I was a bubbling drain.

'Yara,' she murmured, finally pulling away.

Her eye whites glowed amber. Orange sun streamed through a screen.

I thought, she was the actress. She had the face for it, not me.

'You want me? What do you want? Sometimes it's hard to tell.'

I felt all my tongue's muscles from our kissing: plant stems, fireworks. I wished I could just shoot a big gush everywhere.

'Come back,' I said. 'Kiss.'

I couldn't speak right. But she smiled and smashed her mouth back onto mine. I stretched my tongue up inside her as long as it went. I saw a pestle and mortar, my grandmother's collection. Her entire set on display from Switzerland. I thought, pestles and mortars are penises in cups. I pulled her head to the left. I was scared for a second of feeling like a man. With my hand threaded through her hair, she lifted her baggy white shirt. She bit the collar to keep it pinned up. I thought she looked like a boa with shimmering scales. Her tits, tea-soaked sugar cubes. Her nipples, big as grapes.

My lips felt so raw. I looked down between us.

'Don't be scared,' she whispered. 'Don't be scared of anything.'

Her panties were see-through. Little red threads emerged like hairs from the sides. I thought, my mother will never know what I'm doing right now.

Then she took both my wrists and stuck my hands on her breasts. They felt weirdly like clay: half-spongy, half-stiff. And she ballooned her T-shirt around the back of my head. Her head was outside. It was hot under there. I thought, make her cry. She shimmied toward me, on my lap. Her breasts moved too fast. She was lost in her feeling. I wanted to be lost in mine, too. I felt pins and needles all over me, even my tongue. A string of saliva stretched between us, gummy and loose like a bridge. Her breast touched my face. I groaned and grabbed the nipple with my teeth. I thought, calves suck their mommies. Grass glistened outside. I felt a rake raking down in my shorts. I kept trying to bite. It felt so good to suckle. My throat swelled at the back. I realized I was having sex for the first time. My whole body was swelling as if I'd been stung. I knew that I couldn't tell anyone.

We kept going like that for so long, with me under her shirt. When she finally unsheathed me, she lifted my crop top. She stared at my bra: a black tank top, the ugly sports kind.

'Let's take this off,' she said, helping me out.

The rim was elastic. The bra twisted over my head. I felt embarrassed without it. I was a girl, not a man. She looked down, her eyes narrowed. She was still on my lap. My breasts were bigger than hers. I didn't know what she thought about them. She suddenly pushed them together from the sides into one.

'Okay,' she said quietly, making a big, slippery balloon on my chest.

The skin between my breasts squeaked. My nipples felt like knots tied too tight.

'Come on, lie down.'

I must've unzipped my own shorts. I was lying down on the couch. She was sitting on me, straddled. I felt her scratchy red panties against my pubic bone. I could feel her thick vulva. My underpants matched my sports bra. I think I was breathing too hard. I had to half-close my eyes. My shorts were pinned at my ankles. I felt like I was tied up with rope. Then she was stroking me high up – I mean higher between my thighs. I started breathing even harder. I wanted to look down but I could not lift my head.

'Let me touch you,' she said.

She seemed so intense. My panties felt too thin. Her fingers felt so big. Or maybe it was just that the outside and inside of me felt exactly the same. Swelling, pulsating, and ticklish like fur. My head pinned to the couch pillow; it felt anchored there. I kept feeling her vulva. I kept feeling rope burn.

'Yara,' I heard her say. 'I love this so much.'

She put two fingers down there, one on each lip. Then she twisted my underwear to the side and I gasped. Her thumb rotated upward. I felt a balloon grow inside. Fireballs. Maelstrom. All five fingerprints.

'Can you feel me?' she asked, leaning into my ear.

'Mmm,' I got out.

Her fingers were crossed like two roots. She pushed them deeper inside, fixed knuckles, soldered and hard. I felt so weird. I didn't know how to relax. She started sucking on my neck as she pushed inside me. Suddenly, everything sped and I bucked up into her. Torpedo fast. I lifted into her hand. My body made slapping sounds. I got so huge and so red. She said, 'Come on, Yara, keep going, keep going, don't stop.' I tightened everywhere. I felt myself slapping her wrist. I squeezed my eyes shut. I saw a crab scuttling into the surf. 'Come on, yeah, baby, come on, go all the way.' Her hard fingers twisted, her body crashed into me. I seized. I heard grunts. I didn't know where I went. I sank through the couch. Only her fingers were real. In a big prickling rush, I was gone from the room. Her hook lured me back. I heard myself pant.

'You are amazing,' she whispered. 'Yara, you are pure fucking sex.'

Then she flattened herself on me, rubbing her breasts to my breasts. She never took her fingers out. I had a whole world down there. I mean, I had a heart and a ragged thigh bone. Since the nose job, this was the first time I'd cried. I wanted to kiss her really badly but my nose had plugged up. She kept pulsing me, stroking, I felt more foam and more swells. Her eyes were so wide right near mine that they looked malformed.

'I love this,' she said. 'I love it so much.'

She repeated herself. I wanted her fingers to do it again. I wanted to burst. I wanted more. But I needed to get up. I needed to blow my nose. Where were my clothes? I felt like I couldn't move. She climbed off me. The room was violet, too dim. I watched her light a cigarette and straighten her long T-shirt.

'Are you okay?' she asked again. Why was she asking me that?

I heard the mewl of that cat. My whole head felt afflicted, like lightning had passed through.

'I should go now,' I said, sitting up, not able to breathe.

My vagina was a big sticky doughnut smashed into the couch.

'You need help standing up?'

I shook my head and slid down to the floor. My bra and my crop top were under the couch. Her smoke hung in the room like a cumulus cloud. I slowly did up my bra and put my clothes on.

'I'm gonna call you a car.'

'I'm not allowed to take cars by myself.'

My eyelids twitched like caterpillars. I didn't remember how I'd walked to the park.

'Come on, Yara. Where do you live?'

My bra felt all coiled and wet on my back.

'You shouldn't be walking alone around here at night.'

I remembered I'd walked to Mindu Park on the street full of butchers. I remembered the sharp floral gates in a slope on her street. I still felt her knuckles shoved up inside me.

'Tell me where you live,' she said, pulling me upright.

'Adrianópolis,' I said. 'With my mom. In Cristal Tower.'

'I'll call you a car, rich girl,' she said, untwisting my bra strap, not missing a beat.

I'm not rich, I thought. My grandmother in São Paulo was. My mother moved north when she was pregnant with me. My mother worked as a law clerk. Glorified secretary, she sometimes said.

'I don't want to take a car.'

'Okay, I'll walk with you then.'

'No!' I said, louder than I meant to. 'I just need to go home.'

'Then you will call me when you get there, so I know that you're safe.'

Her tone reminded me of the babysitters I'd had as a kid.

I couldn't look her in the eyes. I really needed to leave. She unlatched the lock of her front door. She kissed me good-bye on the cheek. For some reason, that kiss felt like she was punishing me.

I ran down her sloped, dirty street thinking about my mom being mad. I heard a dog's bark, but there were no dogs around. She'd had her fingers inside me. I was running downhill. Men listened to radios, leaning against cars. I tried to pull down my crop top so it covered my waist. I thought about my math test. I tasted incense.

I think I walked for an hour. The sky was bruised black. Birds touched their beaks on the telephone wires.

My mother heard me come in from the balcony. She half stepped inside through the screens, one arm out the door to keep her cigarette alight.

'Well?' she said, smiling, looking me up and down.

I knew she thought I'd just been with a guy.

Her smoke rose there violet, helix-like.

I wanted to tell her that I'd just sucked a woman's tits. But my heart was beating too fast.

Mom, I have a dick.

✦

The Sea of Galilee was actually a lake.

'Get dirty,' said Aloni. 'Then you wash off on the beach.'

He looked at me in my red string bikini. The Canadian girls wore sports bras and bathing suit shorts.

I'd gone down at two in the morning to the computer console. The screen looked bubble-shaped, like a little pregnant robot. The letters on the keyboard were in both English and Hebrew. I took a beer from the bar fridge and sat down to log in.

I wish I could lick you, I wanted to type into AOL chat.

The computer hummed like an industrial fan.

My mother had hugged me so hard at the airport. I knew she was relieved I was actually getting on the plane. My girlfriend had been scheming for months to get me to move in. At home, sometimes I'd do nothing but go between my bed and the fridge. My mother said, I can't control what you do with your life, but you know I don't agree.

Shalom, I wrote, letter by letter on screen.

I saw Manny's handle appear: 666Devilman. I gathered my knees up into my long Birthright T-shirt. There was a hole at the back of the desk for the computer's cluster of cords. The hard drive blew a weird heat. I knew Manny would see me, text her. Manny was from Itacoatiara, like her. He understands me, my girlfriend always said.

I miss you, I typed, waiting. Then I quickly backspaced.

I hated Manny. I hated him so much. A timer on the screen showed fifteen minutes counting down.

Maybe *I miss you* had been channelled. Maybe missing was not what I felt. I mean, my whole life with my girlfriend had been so feelings-based. But I don't think I ever knew what I specifically felt. I remembered my beer. I drank it almost half down in one pull. It was like I'd been stuck for so long in a pattern of anticipating her pain. She always had all this disappointment when I couldn't tell her how I felt. Her eyes showed so much hurt when I couldn't say *I love you* out loud. She squinted and blinked. Her face created tension in a snap. I mean, one wrong little thing like not saying *I love you* in the morning and the pain right there under the surface flowed outward like sap.

If I didn't feel like saying *I love you*, why was it such a big deal? Why did she have to ruin a whole day with her tears?

She was the youngest one in her family. She had four older siblings. Her parents, she told me, drank every night. She said she felt like a container for their dysfunction growing up.

Our house was a zoo, she said. There was no room for me.

My girlfriend lay her head in my lap while I raked my fingers through her hair. Sometimes I felt older than her. She didn't believe that me and my mom didn't fight. I think she was jealous that I was an only child. She knew I did really well at school, that I had a grandmother in São Paulo who bought me jewellery and clothes. I think my girlfriend was jealous that my mother made sure I learned English. Sometimes, to bypass her jealousy, I told her that I hated my mom. Or I hated my mom with all her boyfriends, the steady stream of men in and out of our place. When the truth was, I was sort of impressed. I mean, I don't think I ever doubted that she loved me the most.

'I just need to hear you say *I love you*,' said my girlfriend one morning, five minutes after waking up. 'That is a really normal thing to need.'

My girlfriend believed there was a reason I was 'avoidant.' I think she thought she knew me better than I knew myself. I did feel guilty a lot. I wasn't sure where that came from. I know I felt sort of guilty that I hadn't told my mother about her. I felt sort of guilty for lying. Guilty for not wanting to tell anyone about her. I was stuffed up. Feelings, shit, feathers. I didn't know what I felt. I didn't care that me and my mother never said *I love you* out loud.

'It's hard to ask someone for something you want, you know that? Something as simple as *I love you*, and you can't even do that.'

'I do, though. I love you,' I said quietly.

I didn't want the whole day to circle around this.

Morning and night, I got in the habit. *I love you. I love you.* I said it even when I didn't feel it.

I wrote into the flashing chat line: *I don't think I'm coming back.*

It was eight o'clock at night the day before in Manaus. She should've been in front of her computer waiting for me.

I wanted to know: did she think it was illegal what we had done? Did she believe fifteen-year-old girls had to be welcomed into sex?

I backspaced. I couldn't ask her.

It wasn't illegal. But when did my feelings for her start to change? When did I stop feeling turned on, wanting to touch her, have sex? Or maybe I didn't ever not want to be with her. Maybe sex was the way I felt love.

Where are you? I wrote and pressed Enter finally.

She wanted us public. She wanted me to come out. She said it was my turn. She said I had to tell my mom.

When her handle appeared, my fingers looked like spiders' legs over the keys.

Where the fuck have you been?

Knuckles like hexes. I felt totally numb.

I had to call your mother.

Don't call her!!! I typed. My hands had descended, full of alarm. My mother hated my girlfriend. At some point, my mother knew. I didn't have to tell her. She'd seen me and my girlfriend on Cristal Tower's pyramid steps. All my mother said was, Yara, it's your life, but I do not understand.

I couldn't believe she'd called my mom.

I haven't fucking slept at all since you left. Not even an hour.

I think I wanted to go back and live from fifteen years old again. I would never have called her. We would never have had sex.

I want to die Yara. I miss you so much.

Tal said that my girlfriend should be arrested on her thirtieth birthday.

I hate this world, she kept typing. *I want it to end.*

My heart beat triple time. The beer made it worse.

Your mother told me to leave you alone.

I thought, I need money from my grandmother. I need money to stay away.

I should've listened to my mother. I'm sure she was furious.

I can't sleep. I can't eat. I can't go to work. I am in so much pain, Yara, without you right here.

Did my mother hang up on her? Did she utter a curse? What if my girlfriend quit her job at the clinic and got on a plane to Israel?

I should've just mimicked her feelings and told her I wished I'd never left. I should've typed *I love you.* I needed to type something back.

I have five minutes, I wrote slowly, fingerprints in every key.

I was sweating. I needed to stop talking to her.

A banner started flashing onscreen in Hebrew. It was a picture of brown leather sandals pigeon-toed at a waterfall.

Get a card and call me. Right now. I need to hear your voice.

Don't waste your life with that woman, said my mother for the one thousandth time.

An Israeli soldier just got abducted, I wanted to type. Three Palestinians died.

I miss you so much. I want to fucking die.

I saw their dead bodies. I saw Frankenstein. Her pain was out of proportion.

There's no phone around, I typed.

Feelings, I thought, are like sleights of hand.

I miss kissing you. I miss fucking you. I miss your tongue inside me.

The counter ticked down. I got up, wobbling. I wanted more beer from the fridge. I thought, she doesn't know what I am doing. She can't see me. My kneecaps were hot from the hard drive. I stuck my tongue in the cold bottle neck. My cunt was a periscope: it could see what skimmed up on the surface of the pond. I thought, maybe I only feel love when I am just about to cum. When my ear channels expand, as if they are going to pop.

My mother gave me this ticket. My mother fixed my face.

Tal said my body knew what was wrong.

Can't you feel it, Yara? I am fucking suffering.

I realized with some kind of certainty that I wasn't going home.

You hate me, my girlfriend typed.

I don't hate you, I typed back.

Don't lie. I know you're relieved to be so far away.

There were only thirty seconds left. She was going to be thirty next week.

I thought, the world has no end. It didn't end on 9/11. It didn't end with my nose job.

I'll kill myself if you don't return.

Then the computer screen flashed and sandals filled the whole screen.

I love you.

Sex offender. Tal wanted to sue.

I felt like the rabbit, trapped in a field full of blood.

✦

I packed my backpack before Tal and Reena woke up. My head felt like smashed cardboard from the beers I drank last night. I sat beside Jonah on purpose on the bus.

'Aren't you going to call your parents?' he asked, cupping his phone in both palms.

Jonah looked like that actor Sean Penn.

'Jonah's dad paid so that he could log in from here.'

Joel was sitting across the aisle from us. His face was all freckled. He reminded me of a gnat.

'Israel now has a mediator through Egypt,' Jonah reported. 'To find out how Gilad's being treated, if he's still alive.'

'The whole country's hanging on.'

'He's being named "Israel's lost son."'

Aloni tapped the mic from the front of the bus. 'Birthright, if we need a cause for a little celebration, Tzfat is next!'

Jonah stared at the mushy, hot smash of my thighs.

'Tzfat has been Jewish since the thirteenth century. Once you visit, once you see it, you will never be the same.'

'My mother,' I said to Jonah, 'doesn't worry about me.'

Tal and Reena sat three rows up. I was trying to forget about my girlfriend threatening me with her death.

'I want to film something,' I said. 'Can I use your phone?'

'You want to make movies like Tal?' Jonah said, as if I was copying her.

What I wanted, in fact, was to add another line to my pitch: *On my sixteenth birthday, my girlfriend filmed us having sex. She thought our sex was spiritual and we could heal people with it.*

On the bus, it felt like Tal could feel me defecting from the path of the law. What was 'illegal,' I wanted to tell her, was not sex with an age difference or sex being filmed. What was illegal, I wanted to say, was the fact that my girlfriend had been manipulating my feelings for years. She'd been coaxing out my feelings, turning them into a paste. She'd been making little patties of my feelings so that she could feast!

I fell asleep on Jonah's arm. He roused me when we got to Megiddo and Magdala. He said we had to choose one site to explore and meet back at the bus in forty-five.

Jonah said I could use his phone any time.

There was an ankle-height maze of stones marking the house in Magdala where Mary Magdalene was born. Artifacts had been arranged on a table under a modern-looking outdoor barn. Tal came with me to Magdala. We walked side by side. I thought, I have not been sexually exploited. I have not been traumatized.

A speckled white statue of Mary loomed in the centre of the site. Me and Tal walked together in and out of the barn. The sun was so hot it felt painful, separating hairs in my scalp.

'My girlfriend's friend Manny was the one who said we could make money from the sex tape.'

'So, a dude was the director? Oh my God. It gets worse.'

I remembered how Manny came so close up behind me, how I cranked my head back to look. He had dark brown nipples that looked like walnuts. He'd abandoned the camera, let it run on its own. I remembered my body rippling as he came near us. I remember how I forgot about my girlfriend. His cock lay on his stomach like a cross.

'Did you fuck him on camera?'

'Once I did, yeah.'

Tal seemed hardened and stressed – more so-called illegality. But I stayed in that room with them. I didn't kick the tripod.

I didn't know how to tell Tal that Manny was unimportant.

Manny never told me where he put the sex tape. Manny squeezed his crotch like a fistful of clay.

Turning on the masses. The art of magical broadcast. People need to fucking move, my girlfriend said. Wake up their tails. This is the definition of healing, Yara: deep total change. You see love like ours onscreen and you want it for yourself.

Megalomaniac, said my mother. That woman is a total narcissist.

I was pulled between my mother and my girlfriend trying to have a hand in who I was.

✦

The sky was blinding, empty blue. We walked in single file up a steep, brick, one-way road.

'Taglit, we have thirty-two synagogues in one long city block. You breathe in, you feel history!' Aloni shouted.

The bricks looked like potatoes. Me and Tal stayed apart. Our group gathered in a semicircle at an iron gate halfway up the hill. The house behind the gate looked like it was from a fairy tale. The roof was made of horsehair, the door painted bright green.

'This is my favourite day of Birthright,' Aloni said, herding us into the hut.

Inside, the floors were uneven. It smelled like papier-mâché. There were posters on the walls with Hebrew letters drawn in calligraphy. Rows of burgundy books on recessed shelves locked behind medieval-looking, bubbled glass doors. Velvet theatre ropes led us into a backroom.

'Check out the Judaica, relics of lost life,' Aloni gushed.

It was a kind of sanctuary in the back, where criss-crossed rafters held up a dome. Aloni gestured for us to all sit on the rotten wood floor. Candelabras, burnished in the joints, were stuck to the walls. Bibles on pedestals. It smelled like mushrooms and armpits. My kneecap touched Jonah's. My flip-flops bent in the floor. Then a bearded man in a floor-length black robe walked into the room. He tripped on his hem as he stepped over Aloni into the middle of us.

'Birthright,' he said. 'Birthright, where have you come from?'

The man looked like a father. His beard was a web. His accent was from America, nasal and crude.

'Here lie Rebbe HaKohen, Rebbe Vitale, and Rebbe Esperanssa,' he said.

I wasn't sure if he meant literally, like, if this was a crypt.

'Rebbe Berab, Rebbe Ashkenazi, Rebbe Gallico, and Rebbe Tzahalon … '

Then the man spread his arms and started spinning around.

'Birthright, the great rebbes are here for you all.'

The man opened his mouth, as if to sing. He pulled up the hem of his robe so that he didn't trip. He had long, jointed arms and a moon-shaped belly. He told us he was Rabbi Fishman, a native Philadelphian.

Tal looked at me strangely and I knew it right then: she'd called her parents in Toronto and told them about me.

'Your girlfriend groomed you,' Tal had said. 'She exploited you. There is no way around that.'

I saw copper-coloured crucifixes pinned on all the store walls back home. Rabbi Fishman started singing in Hebrew as he pivoted around like a pin. Groomed, scratched, and stroked. That's just how I grew up. Suddenly, accordion music was piped into the room.

Aloni jumped up and ran into the circle with Rabbi Fishman.

'Dance, Birthright, dance! You are waiting for what?'

I stood up first as Aloni and the rabbi twirled together with crossed and locked wrists. The floors creaked. Chords coloured the walls of the room. The rafters were criss-crossed and multi-plying. Aloni's bare feet were covered in soot. He unclasped hands with the rabbi and started pulling kids up one by one. I was smiling. I was jumping. I felt my flesh shake.

'Brasilia is the best Jewish dancer we have!'

We were all spinning in a circle, doing the hora. I scoured the circle for Tal, but she wasn't there anymore. The rabbi was craning and nasal. *Yadda-dee, yadda-dum.* I spotted Reena, brow furrowed, bouncing across the line. All of Birthright was forced to hold hands and spin as fast as we could. I'd done it with my grandmother before. I felt everything inside me jiggle and burn. My flip-flops pounded the wood. I thought, joy is passed on.

At the hostel near the Dead Sea, we sat on a fissured concrete patio strung with Christmas lights. Our table had a stained, browning map of the world in laminate.

'Israel says it could release hundreds of prisoners in exchange for Gilad,' Jonah read off his phone.

'That is a very poor idea. Those are murderers,' Joel said.

'Yeah, well, the Palestinians understand their Machiavellian bargaining piece.'

'Bro, what does that mean in English?' Joel said, winking at me.

'Machiavellian means you're their pawns.'

'Hold up. Who's *they*? Who you talking about?'

Jonah set down his phone on the laminated map. 'I mean Israelis, bro. Politicians. Whoever's making these deals. They think one Jewish life equals *thousands* of Palestinians'.'

Joel started laughing, freckles disappearing into creases at his eyes.

I wished I was at the table with Tal and Reena and the rest of the girls. We hadn't spoken since Tzfat. I thought Tal was mad because I didn't agree that what had happened with my girlfriend was illegal.

'Yo, dude. My dude. This is the whole reason we are here! To get it through our thick skulls that we are one and the same. Israelis and Jews, Jews all over the world. We Jews have a different understanding of the preciousness of life.'

Jonah slid his hand under the table to mine. His fingers were cramped, the knuckles all dry.

'Preciousness,' Jonah said. 'Bro, what does that even mean?'

They were like tomcats, bitch-fighting, Tal was totally right. Joel sighed and looked at me, dramatically swigging his beer.

'Okay, Miss Brasilia, I'll spell this out for your man. Before the wall was built, there were suicide bombers in Israel every week. Café Moment, Café Sbarro, Hebrew U. Those people do not have the same respect for life as you and me. And these are the men that they want to release!'

'C'mon, bro, Palestinians, even the ones in prison, are not all suicide bombers,' Jonah said. 'There has to be diplomacy at some point. There has to be a compromise.'

Joel swigged the dregs of his beer, then dropped the bottle in the sand. 'Back me up, Brasilia. I think we both know that these people are plotting our extermination, correct?'

'That is fucking hyperbolic, bro! The prison system is corrupt.'

Joel started to laugh. 'You're deluded. And why's she so quiet? Can you tell me that?'

I imagined my girlfriend here, arguing with them. She'd tell them about Brazil's military coup in '64. She'd say, Guerrilla warfare is executed by people like you and me. You would fucking fight, too, if you were occupied, right? Think about your own mother or father disappearing for speaking their mind. Politicians just do what they want with the military backing them. The country of Israel is run by military rule. You can't fucking hold an entire people down. In Brazil or Palestine or the rest of the world.

'She's cool. Yara's cool, bro. Everything's good.'

I could feel Jonah's hand pulsing inside my palm. He'd ordered a twelve-pack of beer from the kibbutz commissary.

We'd visited Kibbutz Samar earlier in the day and watched workers milk cows, dig up onions, pack boxes of dates.

'The history of Israel,' Aloni had narrated, 'is tied to tilling the land. Bundists and Socialists have been here since the dawning of the twentieth century. These people stuck shovels in earth to found their patch of promised land.'

We'd walked past a tilted old farmhouse that doubled as a dorm. A man held a matted washcloth over a bucket and doused his armpits. All the workers were Thai. They laid dates in boxes, rapid-fire.

'Come on, Brasilia.' Joel smiled. 'Bless us. Tell us what you think. One thousand Palestinian terrorists in exchange for Israel's lost son Gilad.'

'Hey, bro. I said to leave her alone.'

I pulled my hand out of Jonah's.

'I think it's stupid,' I said. 'It's not going to work.'

'Aha!' Joel wiggled his ass in the chair. 'The Girl from Ipanema speaks!'

I noticed that Tal and Reena in the corner were doing shots.

'The "preciousness of life" or whatever you want to call it,' I said, 'is just one end of the axis – on the other end is suicide and death. Jewish people don't have a monopoly on preciousness, or whatever you said …'

'Oh yeah, Brasilia, don't stop. Jonah, she's on a roll.'

I wanted to punch this gnat right in the nose. Everyone who read anything knew about the randomness of death. Especially in true crime, I mean, that was its point. A woman with her fetus cut out of her – there was no reason for that. Being strangled with your own blouse. You can't control violence.

'The preciousness of life means don't treat someone like a thing. Like, it's an accident, it's random, that you're on this side of the wall and they're over there. You can't hold an entire population down by force. You're not better than the Palestinians and neither am I.'

Joel laughed. 'Uhhh, Brasilia? Lemme stop you right there. It's not random who was born a Jew. We're Chosen, capital C. You won the fucking lottery. You should start acting like it.'

'Yo, bro,' Jonah warned.

I stood up. I believed what I said.

Joel looked at Jonah. 'You are pussy-whipped, dude.'

I walked out of the bar on the shifting sand floor. Jonah followed me closely. I knew Tal watched us leave. I didn't win the fucking lottery. Joel wasn't smarter than me. When people are being battered, they have to fight back. But what if Joel was right that violence wasn't random, being Jewish wasn't random. How could that be? I started spiralling thinking about suffering. What if my girlfriend was really suicidal? Would she actually kill herself?

'Ignore him,' Jonah said. 'Are you okay?'

We veered through the hostel's topsy-turvy sand paths, which were covered with thin bamboo mats. Jonah walked close behind me, trying to keep up. I remembered all the books I'd read where a man kills his girlfriend, or random women, or where a mother kills her kids. People strangled and battered: failed love at the root. I felt sharp cramps in my gut. I needed to call her right now.

'Do you get AOL on your phone?' I asked Jonah.

'Yeah, if we're in the bus or the city, it picks up a signal.'

A black tarp covered the main walkway. Stars prickled through the rips. All of a sudden, Jonah grabbed my arm and stopped me at a tent pole.

'I like you, Yara. I mean, really. A lot.'

I couldn't say to Jonah I wasn't thinking the same. I needed to talk to my girlfriend. Jonah blocked me with his T-shirt. His head looked like a dinosaur skull dipping toward me. Then his jaw hit my jaw and his hands clawed under my shirt. I thought about the computer. I thought, my girlfriend hates me so much. Jonah pinched my nipples, his fingers like automotive clamps.

'Stop. I need to call home. Something happened,' I said.

I took Jonah's hands off my breasts.

'Sorry,' he said.

He looked sheepish. The sand was red-lit. I told him we'd sit on the bus tomorrow. I scuttled around him and went back to the bar. Tal and Reena and the girls were all gone. Aloni sat by himself, sucking smoke from a pipe attached to a vase on the floor.

Socialists will run this country again, he'd said at the kibbutz. Stray dates like old thumbs rolled around in the hay.

There was a bald patch on his head in the shape of a coin.

What if I had a penknife and stabbed him? I thought.

Visions of death kept being born in Israel.

There was no computer at the front desk in this hostel like in Tiberias. I ran back through the red sand, along another pathway. I didn't remember which fucking door was our room, each door had a red flap of fabric, each door was a ruse. I thought, I have been blind and now I can see. I knew that, in Israel, something was happening to me. Leaving my girlfriend had not been right. I was worried about suicide. I was thinking about murder and death. Bombs arced like fireworks, dead men hoisted aloft. I finally found Tal and Reena huddled on a saggy double bed.

'I'm stupid, I'm sorry,' Tal said when she saw me.

'Shhhh,' Reena said, holding a barf bag at Tal's chin.

'Yara, I didn't mean to push a fucking narrative of victimhood on you ... '

A *narrative of victimhood*. I froze on the sand.

It all suddenly came together, like a warping black braid: Israel, my girlfriend, the plight of the scapegoat. The narrative of victimhood could be pushed. Like a drug!

'Do either of you have a cellphone?'

My teeth chattered violently.

'It's only for emergencies.'

'Oh my God, Reena, don't be a bitch.'

My teeth felt like stalagmites jutting out of my gums.

The Narrative of Victimhood starring Yara 'The Scapegoat' Yavelberg.

Tal pitched forward and bolted to the bathroom, hand over her mouth.

'Fuck,' Reena said, searching in her backpack on the floor.

She lobbed me her phone and ran to Tal in the bathroom.

The phone was hot in my palm. I felt chaos inside. The loop and pull of my girlfriend. Was she still alive? I'd never called anywhere long-distance before. I had to try a bunch of times, entering the little numbers on Reena's ribbon-sized screen. I had to be quick. I kept making mistakes. It was the middle of the night here, eight o'clock at night the day before over there. The phone started to ring.

'Hello?'

I sat down. I stood up. My voice sounded timid, unknown. The barf bag Reena held had blown under the bed.

'Yara?' she warbled.

All of a sudden, I felt like I was back down on the floor at her place at fifteen years old, fucked-up and scrambling around for my clothes.

'It's me,' I said, feeling like I was going to cry.

'Yara. You called. I was waiting for so long.'

I was relieved she was fine. I felt really weird.

'I'm using this girl's phone. It's not a pay phone. I'm in the desert,' I said.

I felt like I was babbling. There was static. She didn't respond.

'Can you hear me?'

A beetle marched through the bamboo at my feet.

'Manny rented a rooftop for my birthday,' said my girl-friend. 'I'm going to be a DJ.'

She was a pinprick in the fabric, so far away.

'Yara, it's expensive!' Reena yelled through the wind, from the john.

'Who's that?'

'Girls on Birthright. From Canada. They're cool.'

The static hit my face like grits of sand in the air.

'I need you to come home.'

'I have to give this girl back her phone.'

'Stay on the line.'

'I can't.'

'Don't hang up, Yara. Don't you dare.'

My resolve to be separate felt totally gone.

I thought, victimhood is a story that predicts your future.

'I want you back beside me, Yara. I miss you so much. You'll be there for my party?'

'Yes,' I said.

'You promise?'

Fuck. How many days did I have left? *Scapegoat* meant I was cursed. All my weeds would be poisoned. I had no country. No love.

All of a sudden, Reena was behind me and poked her finger into my back. I was so startled I let the phone drop. I watched her pick it up from the bamboo, press a few buttons, and just turn my girlfriend off.

'Wait!' I yelled. 'Why did you do that?'

Reena ran back to the bathroom with her phone. I heard her crying to Tal. I started pacing in the sand. I didn't know why I was digging this hole for myself. Why I said yes.

Your pussy has teeth, my girlfriend used to say.

She had two fingers inside me with lit-up fingerprints.

'Yara, I want to feel your little circle squeeze me.'

I remember my muscles everywhere, pulsing, wanted to do what she said. I used to love feeding her, holding her head. When I was on top, I tried to be weightless and huge. Yara, she moaned, jiggling ropes between us. Ropes of saliva, criss-crossed and tied.

On the phone in Israel, I swung on the bridge between us. Her tongue licked my tears. Wind scratched through the tarps.

I was scared of life without her. I wanted her to leave me alone.

✦

I stood with Tal in a roadside Dead Sea bathroom stall. We had clay on our faces, sand in our wet hair. I'd borrowed Jonah's phone. Tal held it up and moved it around. She cursed and kept circling, turning it side to side. The sun flashed. We were laughing. The Dead Sea made us high. We were slathered with minerals: sun-drunk, lizards of light.

In the open-air bathroom, catching power on the phone, Tal showed me a grainy clip of two people fucking on a couch. I couldn't see their faces clearly. They looked black-and-white.

'Even Reena, I swear to you, is hot for this guy.'

The little video kept switching from bird's-eye to close-up.

'Josh Dee made porn fans out of all girls.'

My bathing suit bottoms sagged with the murk of dead sea.

'I mean, this guy acts consciously, on purpose, how girls want guys to be. He eats them out and then fucks them with their hands behind their back.'

Tal got so serious. I felt like we were soldiers, camouflaged. I'd never heard of Josh Dee, the American porn star. He had his hands around a girl's neck, licking and kissing it. The Dead Sea was half-warm. The girl writhed like a caught fish. I still felt the sting of the salt and the slap of the sun on my scalp. I thought, maybe me and my girlfriend had life-and-death sex.

'Yara, you know everyone says you have the best body on this trip.'

My nipples burned. I felt my girlfriend's hands on my neck. I closed my eyes and I saw her. I was the cause of her suffering.

Me and Tal watched Josh Dee flip the girl over and fuck her doggy-style.

'Hustler,' whispered Tal.

I remembered when I thought I was growing a dick. I felt it in my bathing suit bottoms like a phantom limb. The video switched then, from wide-angle to close-up. Tal turned the volume up so it was louder than the wind. Josh Dee's cock was headless. It made sluicing sounds, pumping in. The girl's vulva got thinner, accommodating it. We heard panting, her panting: low, on repeat. The subsonic fucking was mesmerizing. After a minute, it was as if her pussy seized. There was some kind of expulsion. The penis shot out like a dart.

Tal started laughing. 'Oh my God, did you see?'

I saw that girl's vulva change form – from oval to elephantine.

People entered the bathroom. The girl kept panting uncontrollably. Tal turned the volume down, frantic. I wanted to see that again.

Tal whispered, 'I'm telling you, Yara, this is the only way I'll watch porn. If the girl is squirting, fuck. You can't lie about that.'

Squirting. Josh Dee wiped his dick like a clown. I remembered licking the sheets underneath my girlfriend, lapping everything up.

I felt myself squirm in the Dead Sea cubicle. So Tal watched porn, but she was critical of it. I just wanted to see it again: that girl's metamorphosis.

✦

In Ein Gedi, yellowed cliffs rose around us like sheets.

'So, Brasilia, you like it here?' Aloni asked, approaching my spot on a rock. 'You know, this week is just a taste of how beautiful the Jewish people are.'

He sat down beside me, rubbing his bronzed, hairless thighs. I felt like I was in limbo, between here and her.

'You could get some of your friends to come to join us. Another Birthright. We already have agents in Argentina. But we could use someone like you. A good girl from Brazil, Land of Amazons.'

Aloni wiggled his eyebrows. He wanted me to stay and flirtatiously spread the good news of Israel.

'You see, you learn Hebrew quick. The alef-bets. You work on a farm and you go to a class. It's all free, Brasilia, our mode of reintegration.'

I could pack dates, bathe in buckets, milk cows on a farm.

'Brasilia, I think you know that Israel is good. Am Yisrael Chai, we say. The nation of Israel shall live!'

It seemed like everyone in Israel had to keep defending it. Aloni and Joel, even Rabbi Fishman of Tzfat.

'You don't have to join the army, Brasilia. Unless you want to. We'd love that.'

Aloni licked his white teeth and swatted a flying insect. I remembered when me and my girlfriend went to protests every weekend to try to stop America from dropping bombs in Iraq. We drew slogans on papers: *No oil for blood!* I remember my girlfriend showed me photos on the computer of a short little woman in camouflage pants smiling over a heap of naked grey men.

'A lot of girls find meaning in the uniform,' Aloni said. 'Meaning in the gun.'

At Ein Gedi, I slipped away from Aloni on the rock. I thought, maybe countries at war needed constant bolstering. Maybe Israel was like America: blustering, warlike.

'Eh, Brasilia,' Aloni shouted after me as I walked to Tal and Reena near the spring. 'You know you are one of us!'

'Don't call me that,' I said, turning. 'My name is Yara.'

✦

We arrived with our sleeping bags at the base of Masada. Each sleeping bag had a marked parking spot.

'I will sound the alarm at 4 a.m. and again until you lazy birds rise,' Aloni announced at the firepit in the centre of our camp. 'You take your water and your day pack. The stars are our friend.'

Tal set up her sleeping bag beside mine. The sky was striped in wobbly magenta, blurring beige. Black birds flew overhead, circling the heat. Aloni, I realized, couldn't look at me.

Everyone brushed their teeth with bottled water and spat out foam on the earth.

In the centre of our camp, Aloni made a giant fire. People burned marshmallows on sticks and sang songs.

'Can you film something of me and Jonah,' I asked Tal at the row of bushes lining our camp.

Tal spit out her toothpaste and tied her hair up in a bun.

'I just need ten seconds,' I said. 'Like, my head in his hands. He said it was fine if we don't show his face.'

Tal looked at me. 'I'm not sure I should get involved in whatever that is.'

I started laughing. 'You already are!'

Crows picked at garbage bins lining the lot. Our toothpaste foams shone. I took Tal's arm. It was clammy. I'd never touched her before.

'I know that you told your parents about me.'

Me and Tal were the same height. I tried to keep her with my eyes.

'I told them because they can help you, okay?'

'You can help me. I want you to.'

'Yara, I don't know … '

I didn't let go of her. I felt really good since I'd told Aloni my name. I felt thoughts come together about why I was here.

'Look, it will help me with not going home.'

My victimhood could be solved, I believed, like detectives solved crime.

I summoned Jonah over from the fire. The singing had stopped. He showed us a new photo on his phone of Gilad Shalit. Gilad was slumped and blindfolded against a stone wall.

'This didn't happen in a vacuum,' said Tal, staring at it.

'If you got captured by the Arabs, Tal, you wouldn't last a day.'

'Yeah, they would rape me.'

'Fuck, that's racist,' Jonah said.

'Zionism is racism,' Tal said, looking away.

'Oh my God, is she really that brainwashed?' Jonah said to me. 'You can't be a self-hating Jew and racist against Palestinians.'

Tal looked like she was going to cry.

Maybe Jonah was right. But I was thinking about Aloni, oily limbs and surfer's vibe, all his needy thoughts roiling from inside to outside.

'Um, I just think that some people in Israel don't question themselves,' I said. 'Like they don't have time for guiltiness.'

Jonah and Tal looked at me for more.

'It's hard to tell in this country who is the perpetrator.' I shrugged.

The moon rose over Masada, skull-like and black-bruised. I felt it land in me: the perpetrator paradox.

✦

My mother named me after a famous Brazilian who she always said it was a shame no one knew. The real Yara Yavelberg was Jewish, from São Paulo. She studied psychoanalysis. My mother said she was beautiful, brave, with brains. The real Yara Yavelberg fell in love with a revolutionary. She ran away with him and fought in armed resistance against the military dictatorship. They organized bank robberies and political kidnappings. The real Yara Yavelberg, said my mother, believed in a free and open Brazil. My grandmother knew her family; they were distant cousins. Yara even babysat my mother a few times when my mother was a little kid. My mother said she always knew that she wanted to name her child after her.

You have a good head on your shoulders, Yara, you're brave and brainy like her. Don't waste a minute of life. Life goes fast, my mother said.

The real Yara Yavelberg was killed in 1971. She was executed by the military alone in her apartment. The military said that she committed suicide, but her family never believed that, even though she had strayed so far from them.

My head would not be wasted, I promised my mom.

Life was so slow. I wanted it to speed up.

I wanted to be tough as rope, braided, resistant like her.

✦

On the ground near Masada, there were piles of dried toothpaste.

'We need more light,' Tal whispered, angling her flashlight at my neck.

'Hold my hair,' I said to Jonah.

My mouth felt like putty. Jonah kept tightening my hair, like he had the reins of a horse.

Muscles fired in my eyeballs. I opened my mouth wide.

I was pixelated, transfigured from Brazil to Israel.

While Tal filmed me at Masada, my real nose grew back.

I was morphing from *victim* into *detective*.

✦

We got kicked off Birthright on day six, right after Yad Vashem. The concrete courtyard sizzled white, around a black memorial slab. Aloni hugged the Birthright girls who cried, one by one.

'It's hard, it's hard, I know, it's hard,' he chanted, sounding like Rabbi Fishman of Tzfat.

In the bathroom of the museum, Jonah had showed Joel on his phone: the sound of my sluicing and his lone, stifled grunt. Aloni had confronted them out of the stall.

We'd all stumbled our way up the cliff face in the dark. When we were on top of Masada, the Dead Sea smoked in the distance. The sun rose like an eyeball, dilated pure red. I felt like I could fly off the table: a steppe eagle, gold-winged.

At the top of Masada, I believed who I could be, alone.

I wanted to feel some omnipotence.

I imagined being my girlfriend: that was her mode.

I felt it, wings out, finally in control.

But later that day, we got to Yad Vashem. A museum for the Holocaust – here, they called the Holocaust *Shoah*. The building was inside a mountain; it felt like the opposite of Tzfat. This was a real crypt. Rows of photos, blue-lit. Fuzzy grey people stood like crows on barbed wire. They were emaciated, lock-jawed, their pyjamas black-striped. I didn't see any women, only men at the fence. Bald heads and gold stars, chairs stuck upside down in the streets. I'd never seen these photographs before, from Auschwitz and Dachau. These photos were nothing like my grandmother's well-dressed family; the little girl with her ringlets on her mother's lap, too big. German men coughed from the ceiling: Raus! Raus! I heard glass crack. Piles of watches like cut chains lay tangled in heaps. You couldn't go near the watches or touch anything. In Yad Vashem, I thought, death doesn't die.

I felt like a ghost walking out of that place. Tal emerged with me, dumbstruck, her neck florid with hives. Aloni smothered crying Reena out in the sun in a hug. When he peeled himself off her, his T-shirt was soaked.

'Yalla, girls, we need to talk.'

Tal and I went to Aloni, who was perched up on a wall. He kicked off his flip-flops. His soles were all black.

Don't waste a moment of life. It goes fast, my mother said.

Those burnished pocket watches of dead people reminded me of sundials.

The story of Masada, Aloni had told us last night, was unique: a sect of breakaway families committed group suicide. He said that they killed themselves rather than be conquered by the enemy to serve. I thought of Gilad blindfolded, his bony seat on the floor. Tal threaded her arm in an L shape through mine. I thought of the dead men lifted up and rivered through the crowd in Gaza. Aloni looked down at us. He cracked all his black toes. I remembered my girlfriend saying how she wanted to die. All those men at the fence and at the funeral, desperately alive.

'So, what were you girls thinking? Tell me, what was inside your piggybank heads?'

Aloni's mouth was distorted. I smelled coconut oil.

'You know we had to take a left turn two days back because of Hezbollah? Our situation was dangerous in the north and we had to skip Kiryat Shemona.'

My gut churned. I'd sent my girlfriend the video from our hostel in Jerusalem. Jonah showed me how to attach it to a message to her AOL account.

'Yara, you were taken advantage of in this video, yes?'

'We did it together,' Tal said, before I could speak.

'Oy vavoy. The entitlement never ends! You girls made our situation worse. This will go in the report.'

I felt like I was learning things at a furious pace. New words flew around me, piling up in my brain. *Dachau, Shoah, oy vavoy.* Was *scapegoat* the opposite of *entitlement*? I was perplexed.

'The two of you, I'm sorry, are going to have to leave.'

Tal exploded. 'No way! I'm calling my father. Oh my God.'

'Your father can't help you.'

I looked Aloni in the eyes. He seemed suddenly dangerous, spraying me with guilt. I wanted to spit on this ground: I'd thought he was guiltless. I was wrong.

'I can't go home,' I said.

'Because your home should be here.'

'Did you even hear what she said?' Tal exploded.

'Look, I'm sorry, Brasilia – I mean, Yara – I liked you a lot. But this is Birthright policy. No propaganda.'

'What?' Tal laughed, incredulous. 'What does that even mean?'

Aloni swivelled his head back and forth between us. 'Girls, you tell me. You don't see any consequences for this?'

'No. We can just erase it,' Tal said.

Aloni laughed, massaging sweat into his neck. 'It could have already been shared! This tape could be used as abuse.'

'Abuse?'

I was strangely breathless.

'Yes, Brasilia. Is this what you know?'

That word followed me like a spider, *abuse*, slipping up walls. I felt sick. I fell silent. I thought, fools give blow jobs.

'Don't worry, Yara,' Tal said quickly. 'We'll work this out.'

'You girls must leave Y'Israel tomorrow. All the papers are signed.'

I thought my mother would kill me. Deported from Birthright. I could not go back to my girlfriend. I'd just sent her the tape. Huffing, nauseated, I thought I could die.

Then Jonah emerged from the museum, jumping up on the same concrete wall. He saw us three talking and heeled like a dog.

'Doesn't he have to go with us?' Tal said.

'No,' said Aloni. 'He didn't start anything.'

'Oh my God,' Tal yelled, spinning. 'Birthright is a farce!'

But I knew the farce was not Birthright. This farce was handmade for me. It went: if you present yourself as a scapegoat, you won't be scapegoated. Not true.

HOCUS POCUS

I arrived in your country August 2006. *Scapegoat* the word followed me from Israel.

While my mother was furious that I'd been kicked off Birthright, Tal's parents were proud of her, waving a sign. WELCOME HOME REBELS it said in all caps on fluorescent pink Bristol board.

'I'm Alan,' boomed Tal's father, pumping my hand. He had copper-coloured hair. He smelled like tomato paste. 'And here is the star of the show: Gabrielle.'

'Hey,' Tal said. 'I thought that was me.'

Tal's mom was rubbing her back in an oblong heart shape.

'Call me Gabby,' she said to me, looking coyly at the ground.

People milled around us, pushing saran-wrapped suitcases on wheels.

'Our daughter has spoken very highly of you,' Alan said. 'We hear you're a Jew from the Amazon, yes?'

'Oh my God,' Tal said, extracting herself from her mom.

Gabby was tall and voluptuous. Her sailor-style sundress hid thick red bra straps. Alan held the pink rebel sign to his chest. I knew that Tal's dad was a lawyer and her mom was the victim of sexual abuse. These people had ensured I got a visitor's visa that was good for twelve weeks. Tal told me I could apply for student papers and get a degree. She said things would work out. I could stay as long as I liked.

'What about rent?' my mother had said when I told her the plan.

'They don't want it.'

'They say that and then they resent you. Just wait.'

The four of us walked through the terminal with Alan in front, dragging the pink Bristol board on the ground.

'We thought *rebels* sounded better than *dissenters*, yeah, Gab?'

'Yes, we thought about those words for a while, didn't we?'

Idiots was the word that my mom would've used.

'It's so busy in the city because of the AIDS conference,' Gabby said.

'Yeah, and Harper says he's not coming in.'

'We don't want him here. He's totally homophobic. A pig.'

'A cat who licks his own tuchus,' Alan laughed.

'It's upsetting to my parents that this is who we're governed by,' Tal explained.

'A shande fur di goyim!' Alan yelled, as he charged up a walkway.

Alan had chicken-winged arms, mottled pink. It occurred to me that Tal's neck hives came from him. I watched Gabby gallop after Alan in her high-heeled sandals. It looked like she was trying to control him by remote.

'They're always like this. I apologize.'

My mother said, Don't be an idiot, Yara. These people are different than us.

Idiot resonated in a way that *dissenter* did not. I was missing my girlfriend's thirtieth birthday this week. I'd sent her the tape that got us kicked off Birthright. It occurred to me in the airport and I didn't know how I hadn't thought of it before: I'd given my girlfriend the gift of my treacherousness.

The glass bridge to the parking lot was stained with white marks.

What the fuck was wrong with me? Why had I done that?

The massive airport parking lot had orange pot lights on the floor. Tal's parents huddled around a sleek black car, its hood up. Alan was trying to shift piles of filing boxes around in the trunk.

'Alan, my God. You knew the girls would have their backpacks.'

Tal's father started snorting, taking out boxes one by one. Both of their good moods had suddenly changed. WELCOME HOME REBELS lay on the oily floor. Tal seemed embarrassed. I didn't feel like a rebel at all. I felt like a predator, an idiot, blood running cold.

In a huff, Gabby took my backpack and shoved it into the back seat.

'So sorry, Yara,' she muttered. 'So sorry about this.'

Tal tried to jam her pack in beside mine but it wouldn't fit. 'Dad, your boxes can't stay in the lot.'

'He's not listening. You know that. Selective hearing, your dad.'

Gabby starting piling Alan's boxes back into the trunk by herself.

'Mom, stop. Let him do that. I'll just lay my pack on my lap.'

Alan stood there reading files, as if he didn't see or hear what was going on.

Dissenter, I thought, meant *idiot* about love. I understood why Birthright had excommunicated me.

Inside the car, with both backpacks wedged between us, I thought of the men's bodies in the coffins on Jonah's phone. Ashkelon rockets, tar-coloured gouge marks. I thought I'd turned a corner in my thinking about my girlfriend, but I hadn't at all. Gabby put on the radio. Alan wound his way out of the garage. My T-shirt smelled rancid. My stomach flip-flopped.

Outside, the sun was foamy and weak. Factories on the highway spewed pus-coloured steam. I didn't want to think about my girlfriend watching the gift of the sex tape. I didn't want to see her pained, squinted eyes watching me suck Birth-right cock. I imagined my mother smoking on our balcony. The car's air conditioning made my sandalled feet freeze. I wished I hadn't done it. I wished I could take it back.

'So, there's a new working group at our office … '

'Dad, now?'

Alan cranked his head around to shift lanes. 'Yeah, so, an offshoot of the old-timey exploitation ring. This explosion of abuse on the web, ever since, what's her name … ?'

'Paris,' Tal said quietly, staring at her hands.

'Right!' Alan bellowed. 'The hotel chain.'

A tanker truck honked. They had planned this, I thought. Gabby held on to the handle at her window, biting her lip.

'Our partners are dinosaurs, Yara,' Alan went on. 'They don't understand. Girls see their idol like that and they become vulnerable all over again.'

Tal stared at her father's hot dog–shaped headrest.

'So, what do you think about Paris Hilton? This problem of sex tapes?'

'Oh my God, Dad … '

Alan looked at me through the rear-view mirror. I held his gaze.

'It doesn't always slide into the criminal, as we say. But with the ubiquity of these phones, Yara, we are seeing something – '

'They are jet-lagged, Alan. Famished. Girls, we can order Chinese.'

'He gets it, I promise,' Tal whispered to me.

I knew that Tal had told her parents I'd been in an illegal sex tape. She'd said I was underage, it was posted on Usenet.

I imagined my mother pitching her cigarette ten storeys down, shooing my pain-addled girlfriend away. My girlfriend crying and screaming. I felt the sickening encroachment of her rage.

Gabby turned up the radio. 'Oh, girls, listen to this.'

On the radio they were talking about delegates at the AIDS conference claiming refugee status in Canada.

'Good news.' Gabby clapped. 'No questions asked.'

'Very good,' Alan added. 'Our people can't waffle on this.'

Alan reminded me of the lawyer who me and my girlfriend had watched on TV talking about 9/11. I couldn't remember his name. He always talked in circles, gesticulating.

That guy knows way more than he's letting on, my girlfriend had said.

Tal kept glancing at me in the back seat over her pack. We'd stayed at a hostel near the beach in Tel Aviv last night. She wanted to play beer pong with some guys from Denmark.

Alan rubbed his leather steering wheel.

'Dershowitz,' I said out loud.

'Oy, so it's true he is known all over the world!'

Tal started to laugh. 'That's my dad's nemesis.'

We need to fight back against the enemy, Dershowitz had said. Enhanced interrogation. Every tool to keep America safe.

That's code for legislating torture, I remember my girlfriend yelled at the TV.

Alan took a long ramp off the highway, trying to glance back at me. 'Yara, you should never be afraid to tell us what you think.'

'We don't usually talk about sex tapes and AIDS off the top,' Tal added.

Gabby laughed. 'Oh yes, we do. Yara, get used to it.'

I remembered Dershowitz's nose tip, thickened and pink. I couldn't follow his arguments about the suspects and Guantánamo Bay. I believed my girlfriend. Tal thought my whole relationship with my girlfriend had been coerced. In their car driving into Toronto, I felt like my memory was faulty, in spurts. Like, maybe I was forgetting some other detail about that tape. The first one, the one when I was sixteen.

'Yara, you like a nice lentil soup?'

'Alan. We told them we were getting Chinese.'

I didn't want to hurt her, I just wanted to break up. Tal reached across her bag to get my attention. She smiled. This fancy, refrigerated car had a trunk full of files. The sun felt like dusty white loops drawn on a chalkboard.

Tal had filmed me sucking dick as revenge. I was pretty sure she'd omitted that part from her mom and her dad.

✦

Before things went sour with my girlfriend, or before I got resentful, or before I suspected that I was being used as her emotional sponge, I didn't care about age, I didn't care about our difference: I was totally, completely, desperately in love.

Sometimes, in her place filled with flowers and incense, it felt like we were members of some hidden world. We lay on the couch, stuck flesh to flesh, the radio on. We spent all day without eating. I followed her to the bathroom like a cat. I put my head on her lap while she peed. I missed her when she went out to buy cigarettes. I wanted her to take me with her, put me on a leash.

My girlfriend grew up in Itacoatiara where her mother made baskets and her father chopped cane. She took me there once when I was seventeen. She said we'd chill at the beach and she'd teach me how to surf. She said that all kinds of rich Euro tourists came there for the waves and to hike. My girlfriend had moved away from home at sixteen. At first, she stayed with an older cousin to clean his place and cook. She told me he helped her apply to cosmetology school. It was mostly about tuition, not about grades. My girlfriend had a little tattoo of an angel wing on her hip. The corners of it bled because it had been done cheap. She told me she knew people back then who sold crack. She told me she'd smoked it once with her cousin and it felt like drowning. It's like drowning in a whirlpool and you're fucking happy about that, she said. My girlfriend told me she knew that if she did it one more time she'd never stop. She would've dropped out, done anything, for more ways to feel that bubbling. It's wicked bubbling, she said, that churns underneath everything.

We took a coach to Itacoatiara and rented a scooter near the terminal. I'd lied to my mother. I said it was grad night away with my class. My girlfriend told me to be careful of the bike's pipe. It could burn off my calf and she wouldn't hear me screaming. I held around her waist. Her skirt flared in the wind. I never felt like anything was missing from her. My girlfriend seemed so solid; an authority on things. I rubbed my face in her back. She smelled like the flesh inside dark purple grapes. Life was speedy with her, thrilling. Back then, she was my life. I didn't care about wicked bubbling. I didn't know about suicidal thoughts. Holding on to her back on the bike in Itacoatiara, it felt like this was all meant to be. I had an older lover, a woman, someone who knew how to live.

Her parents' house was a fifteen-minute ride from our guesthouse on the beach. I don't know why I didn't think about meeting her parents in advance. The house was tiny, sand-coloured, raised up on bricks. My girlfriend was sweating, her hair up in two buns. Yellow buckets around the house made a kind of a fence. I followed her to the backyard, where she propped up the scooter. I smiled at her parents. The bike's kickstand sunk a few inches down in the earth. Her parents were sitting around a little fire. They saw us together and they didn't react. I mean, they didn't even wave. It was almost like we weren't there. The light was going down quickly, they were bulbous, moving shadows on the sand-coloured wall. I thought this was weird. I felt bad. My flip-flops stuck to the mud. When had she seen them last? What had she told them about me? I realized that a bunch of children in diapers in one corner of the backyard were kicking something. My girlfriend gave her mother an envelope and her father a bottle of booze. I stood there behind her. I waved at the kids. It looked like a chicken or some other animal they were kicking around. My girlfriend finally introduced me to her parents by both my names.

'This is Yara,' she said. 'Yara Yavelberg.'

Her mother had a strange smile. I wasn't sure if we would handshake or if I should just smile back. They stayed in their seats like figurines. They seemed the same age as my mother, but weathered and stout. I knew that my mother was well-preserved; all her boyfriends were younger than her. I kept nodding and smiling at her mother, expecting something. But her mother got up and walked away from us to stir some-thing on a hot plate. The air reeked of gas. I was surprised that her parents were both short. Later, my girlfriend told me, her mother thought I was a snob.

Over the years, I thought a lot about that. I'd assumed that night that I'd done nothing wrong. I mean, I thought I was nice, being quiet and saying thank you. But later, it was clear: I didn't understand how to be, I didn't get who they were, I was stiff inside. They sensed it. My girlfriend's mother felt like something about me advertised that. Maybe it was money, maybe my mother and grandmother had insulated me.

My girlfriend drank cana with her father, the stuff that she brought. I kept looking over at her, but the night air was obscuring her eyes. One of the kids started to scream. The chicken had bit him, is what I understood. Mosquitoes buzzed all around us. Her mother was talking too fast. I'd never seen my girlfriend drink cana before. It was liquor made from cane sugar, the cheapest drink in Brazil. After her mother came back from removing the chicken from the kids, she motioned me over to give me a bowl of her soup.

'Thank you,' I said.

She didn't say anything back. I shuffled over to my milk crate burning my fingertips. I heard the revving of cars. I hadn't ever met people like my girlfriend's family before. Chickens scuttling, rangy kids, a backyard full of mud. I had been shuttled between my mother and my grandmother my whole life. Apartments with front desks, baked chicken, clear soup scraped of fat. My girlfriend's family were pardo, mixed black and white. My grandmother once told me that pardo meant a leopard's spots. Inside my soup, two potatoes glowed white. I thanked my girlfriend's mother profusely and I ate way too fast. The soup tasted like goat. My girlfriend didn't eat. I watched her pour shot after shot after shot for her dad. I didn't know how she was going to drive us back to our room at the beach. When we'd arrived at the guesthouse a few hours before, I thought we'd have sex.

Even though the bed sagged and the walls were hospital green. A bucket beside the toilet filled with toilet paper hadn't been cleaned.

'Is breakfast included?' I said, making a joke.

'Let's just get this over with,' my girlfriend said, grim.

The diapered kids with the chicken didn't want to eat soup. My girlfriend had two brothers and a sister. I guessed they'd just dropped off all their kids.

'You want to be a doctor?' her mother finally said to me. 'My doctor's name is Basbaum.'

The fire threw sparks. What did my girlfriend tell them about me? What was I to them?

The darkness descended, sky the colour of mud.

I ate the potatoes, two meat eyes in my soup.

I'd never be a doctor. I just liked to read. I felt so alone in the massive backyard four times the size of their house. Crane-like birds flew low, birds I didn't know. My girlfriend's father seemed sunken. At one point, his hands gave way. Soup spilled on his legs and he couldn't get up from his seat. My girlfriend's mother started yelling and I couldn't under-stand. The kids all got quiet in the chicken-filled corner of the yard. I thought I should go to them, leave her and her parents alone.

I knew I didn't want to be here. I felt sickened by soup.

My girlfriend finally looked at me. 'Let's go,' she said.

I followed her to the side of the house, leaving her mother yelling, all the kids in tears. My girlfriend was cursing, trying to pull the scooter up out of the mud. The sky was dark, drained of stars. Our scooter was stuck. I tried to help her get it out but she pushed me away. She smelled like soaked peaches. I took a step back.

When she finally ripped up the back wheel like a root out of the earth, she laughed and started dragging it back to the road. She leaned on it, hard breathing. Out front, it felt like a forest at night. I did not want to get back on that bike with her. She was totally drunk.

'I'll walk back,' I said.

'Don't be fucking dumb.'

My girlfriend straddled the bike.

'You'll get raped in the bushes. You don't know where you are.'

I was carrying my helmet from the rental. I started walking out the way we came. My girlfriend revved the scooter and rode behind me, clicking gears.

'You'll get raped,' she repeated.

'Don't say that. Shut up.'

I'd never heard her use the word *rape* before.

'You know I can handle my alcohol, Yara.'

I felt mad at her, really mad, for the first time in my life.

'Look at me,' she said, hands off the handles. 'I am motoring good!'

She sped in front of me on the road and did a quick figure eight. Then she drove up ahead. Suddenly, I was all alone in the dark. The ground was alive, ants on my flip-flops. I scratched my legs, looked ahead. I wasn't sure she was ever coming back. Fear flushed through me like ink. Mosquitoes whined in my ears. I walked with my arms out in front of me like coat hooks. I wanted to be home. I had slept with my mother until I was ten. Then I saw a flashing front light, I heard her bike engine hum. I don't know how long she had left me alone. I put on my helmet. She drove up to me. Fuck you, I thought. I kept walking ahead.

'Just get on the bike, Yara.'

I felt like throwing up. My girlfriend stopped. She got off the bike. Then I got on. She tightened my arms around her like a belt. Her T-shirt was soaked. We drove on the dark road, mud air. I had to turn my head to breathe. I saw her father's atrophied hands and the chicken's kicked beak.

My girlfriend drove fast past the lit-up beach strip where we were staying. I saw people dancing on the beach under strung-up Christmas lights. I wanted to be there with them. The road curved away from the beach and we drove up another hill. This one seemed too steep, the leaves too close to my head. We hit a weird, slurry bump on the road and I screamed. I did not want to die here, with tourists smoking crack. I couldn't look left or right. My girlfriend stunk like a donkey. My helmet was stuck.

Eventually, she pulled over at some kind of lookout. Immediately, I climbed off the bike and got away from her raggedy breaths. There was a fence of criss-crossed branches overlooking the sea. I felt so apart. Her mother hated me. Blurry moonlight. The scooter's kickstand didn't work. The bike fell on its side like a corpse.

'Why are you so upset, Yara? Fuck my whole life.'

I didn't want to take off my helmet. I could not look in her eyes. She grew up in that house. She was trying to get away.

'Yara, I need you right now. Why can't you fucking understand that?'

She was right. I didn't understand why I was just thinking of myself. But I didn't want to be here. I needed to leave.

'I'm sorry,' I whispered.

Sorry for not being who she needed. I walked toward the half fence of tied branches. I remembered her hanging gold cross. I wished I'd never got a nose job. I wished I'd said no to my mom.

'See there. That's Saturn,' my girlfriend slurred beside me, pointing left.

I followed her finger at the edge of the cliff. Looking up made me dizzy. It made me afraid.

'Saturn,' she said, 'is malefic.'

My hands felt like hooves on the bark of the fence. I remembered learning in science class that the rings of Saturn were rocks. It was the stormiest planet, full of tornadoes, riptides. The sea rippled down below us. It looked black-and-white. I didn't know if we could make it down the same way we'd come up.

'My mother knows I like girls,' my girlfriend said. 'There is fucking nothing she can do about it.'

She wanted me to tell my mother. She wanted us to live as girlfriends.

'You don't give a shit about me really, do you, Yara?'

The sea rippled in wavelets. The moonlight was cold. I didn't like being accused of no feeling. I didn't know if I felt gay.

'You've never been curious. You don't really care about the way my mind works.'

Why was Saturn malefic? Was it malefic to flee?

The zigzagged cliff fence moved back and forth in the wind.

'Why don't you care about me, Yara? I just want to know why.'

Because your love is conditional, I couldn't say. Booby-trapped.

'Let's just go now,' I said, as calmly as I could.

Suddenly, my girlfriend yanked me and swung me around by the arm hard. I was still wearing my helmet. I tripped backwards, terrified. My girlfriend's hair had unwound. Her breath steamed alcohol.

'You don't love me,' she cried, her jaw cracking wide.

I saw the squat face of her mother grafted onto hers.

My girlfriend slid down to her knees.

'I'm sorry, Yara. I just love you too much.' She pressed her forehead down into the ground near my feet. I unstuck my back from the fence. I didn't want Saturn to plunge down to earth.

'I wish I didn't need you. God, I don't want to be like this.'

I remembered when she told me we were lovers in a past life. She said that I was her mother and she'd been my baby who was sick. That that's why we couldn't separate, that's why I couldn't leave. Especially when she was crying. Her cries got in my head. Mother-baby love is the ultimate, she'd said.

My girlfriend crawled up off her shins and held on to me. She pushed her face into my stomach, kissing it repeatedly.

At the edge of the cliff that night, soaked in her cold sweat, I promised myself that one day I'd escape these rules for feelings that she made.

I wasn't a mother or a baby. I didn't want to be fed.

✦

Tal's house was a bunker. Picture windows jutted out. Black vines decorated the second storey of brick.

'Home sveet home,' Alan said, popping the trunk.

The vines looked half like lace, half like desiccated veins. The porch was supported by two fake marble pillars, sausage pink. Across the street, kids rode their bikes in figure eights.

'Tali,' they screamed, 'when will you babysit us?'

Alan put on Tal's backpack and spun around in a circle for laughs. Gabby linked arms with Tal and they walked up the steps of the front porch. I followed, keeping my backpack on like a shell.

'Tal will show you Josh's room,' Gabby said, inside the hallway, rifling through a velvet-lined box of papers and mail. 'We'll have a feast of dumplings. Yara, are you vegetarian?'

A light fixture hung from the ceiling, with triangular wires.

'Not to worry, Yara. There are oodles of veggie options here!'

She kept repeating my name. It made me feel weird. I followed Tal up the stairs, along a carpeted hallway. We walked past a bathroom and then down a few steps. My toes were numb from the car.

'Are your parents upset that I'm here?'

'Oh my God. No! Why would you think that?'

'Sorry,' I said.

Her brother's bedroom was sunken. It seemed like a second-floor wing. There was a poster of green skulls over the desk and a massive computer screen.

Treachery, deportation, I felt reams of guilt.

'It's clean,' Tal said, pointing to the king-sized, four-poster bed. 'Do not worry about my parents, okay?'

'Can I use his computer?'

'Of course. You can do whatever you want.'

I wanted to take back the tape that I'd sent her. I wanted to find myself on Usenet.

'My mother says we can do our laundry either now or later, okay?'

Josh's bed was made up with a flattened brown quilt. I walked to the window. I thought of the other Josh – the one fucking onscreen.

'Listen to me, Yara, here you don't need to worry about anything.'

I needed to worry. Guilt corroded my gut. I was somewhere in that massive, endless computer where girls humped and sucked and had sex.

'Did you send it?' Tal asked, breathless.

I nodded yes.

'Oh my God, good. That's amazing, Yara. Don't you feel relieved?'

I was supposed to be home tomorrow for my girlfriend's birthday.

There were at least three tapes of me now out there in the world. I was multiplied like Josh Dee and his girls. All through the world, all these fuckers fucking …

You don't shoot sex once. You do it again and again.

Suddenly, Tal pulled me in for a hug. She moved us side to side. I knew Tal believed everything would work out fine. Tal believed things would work out in her life and things would work out in mine.

'Come on, Yara. I thought you were mad.'

'I'm not,' I said, resting my cheek on her neck.

'I guess you just need to settle in a bit, right?'

I felt a lump in my throat that I didn't expect.

'Can you tell me her name?'

Girlfriend, I thought.

'Yara, please. I just want to know who she is.'

Tal peeled herself off me. Her cheeks were all red. I tried to smile, but my lips felt like glue.

I thought, this isn't my life. I am a criminal.

'Look, I'm just happy you're here. We all are. We just want to help. Come down when you're ready. You're safe here, all right?'

I watched Tal walk away. Untouched. Undoubled. Unfucked.

Alone in Josh's room, I remembered the separation wall. The wall that we'd driven by almost two days ago. Aloni had said it had prevented thousands of Jewish deaths.

'If we don't let them in,' he'd said coldly, 'they can't murder us like sheep.'

The wall was concrete, monotone: bars with no air in between. We'd driven past a pentagon-shaped watch tower, panels slanted with black glass. The wall dwarfed our bus. The slabs snaked, tortuous.

'Palestinians can have their own country,' Aloni said. 'On their plot, over there.'

The bus engine rattled. No one said anything, not even Joel.

I thought, the earth has been staked with this unholy wall.

Aloni teetered through the aisle, hanging on to seat heads.

'We won this land, Taglit. War is war. War was won.'

That wall was a template for splitting the world.

'I can't believe they think this is normal,' Tal whispered.

Aloni held his microphone like a comedian.

'Close your eyes, Birthright. Be happy you are young and you are here.'

'What if we're the ones trapped?' I whispered back to Tal. 'What if Fishman fattened us with feed?' What if Aloni is the butcher? What if we're being revealed?'

Josh's desk in Toronto was plywood on top of two orange street barricades.

I didn't want to be callous. I wanted to feel everything.

I turned on the computer from his cracked, black swivel chair.

I had one message from my girlfriend and one from myself.

The fan of the drive spewed heat under the desk. Blood pumped in my ears. I did not understand.

Can't you feel me suffering Yara. I want to die.

File undelivered, my own message said.

I clicked on the blue numbers in my message. Something flashed on and off. Then a black square with a camera appeared on the screen. A timer started counting on the bottom, thirty seconds down. A close-up of the moon suddenly emerged out of black. It was the moon on Masada. The moon in Israel. Then I saw myself in profile, one closed blurry eye. I held on to Josh's desk. Over ten seconds passed. The eye blurred and opened, my whole skull emerged. My forehead was a globe. My nose was a bump. Tal shot my profile like an old movie star. I was glowing. Primeval. Ten seconds I sucked. Velvety, black-and-white, sluicing on tusk.

It was as if a huge weight had been dragged up and out of my chest. My girlfriend hadn't received the sex tape. I felt like I had been saved from more fighting, from more self-sabotage. I could start over. Be a different girl. Now there was space.

✦

The motel on our last night together had really thin walls. We could hear people laughing in a room down the hall. The sheets smelled like bleach. The baseboards, stained with bug spray. A saloon-style light fixture hung near the bed from a painted black chain.

Me and my girlfriend shared rum from the bottle neck. I didn't know how long my mother had been planning Israel. I didn't know how you tell someone that you don't love them anymore.

I-feel-like-we-should-not-be-together sounded so limp, half thought-out.

My girlfriend always used liquor as a precursor. Liquor oils up the neurons, she said. It floods your head with new thoughts. It makes visions appear.

I-feel-like-we-should-not-be-together.

I thought, liquor cracks through denial. Liquor softens the blow.

My girlfriend said Manny was going to meet us at midnight.

I-feel-like-we-should-not-be-together.

It shouldn't be so fucking hard to just speak.

'You're not gone yet, Yara,' my girlfriend said as we kissed.

My heart throbbed way too fast. My body had no brakes. I'd lied to my mother and my girlfriend with the same engorged tongue. That night, a childhood song came into my head from my grandmother's place. My grandmother had records from Israel by a rabbi named Shlomo Carlebach.

My girlfriend asked me to stand in front of her. She asked me to stand there wide-legged.

My grandmother stood and she swayed with the mealy-voiced man. It was some kind of folk song about returning to the land of yourself.

'Yara, bend over,' my girlfriend said, pained.

I-feel-like-we-should-not-be-together.

I was playground equipment. My back was a slide. My girlfriend was making a sigil, a mind drawing, with images not words. I knew this because she'd done it before. She said when you really want something, you have to meditate, pin it down. A sigil is a transformation from real into symbol. It's something you have turned over and over in your mind. It is code.

My grandmother sang the folk song about souls flying home.

My girlfriend lay under my legs. She looked otherworldly, eyes closed. Sometimes, I thought, she looked like a crow. Handsome, eyes orange, her skin had highlights. I loved it so much when she clawed the insides of my thighs. Being looked at like this from underneath by her made me feel weak. Maybe it's true that I was always a natural actress.

My grandmother focused on repetition. Religion and magic were one.

I-feel-like-we-should-not-be-together was caught in a loop.

'One day, the world is going to see you like I do, Yara.'

That girl blows your head up like a balloon, my mother said.

Maybe I was addicted to extreme sexual attention. Maybe I wanted sigils made of me. I could not break up with her. I could not say the words. Alcohol, that night, failed me.

'Stick out your tongue, Yara. Come here. Let me feel it.'

I bent deeper toward her. My tongue, the thickness of shrimp. She held it between her first two fingers and thumb. My girlfriend drew around my lips with my spit.

The more information your body has, the more powerful the sigil is.

I turned myself on thinking this was the last time being trapped in her web. I was leaving in the morning. In nine hours, I'd be on a plane.

I-feel-like-we-should-not-be-together.

My girlfriend slid under my triangle legs and my face. She opened her mouth. She told me to spit. I was naked and feeling. My cunt was a lamp.

I thought, if you do something once, you have to try it again. Every girl had a body. Everyone had a cunt. I smashed down on her body and we suctioned ourselves. Her tongue felt like rapids on the sides of slick rocks.

When Manny arrived at midnight with his camera, I was laid out flat on the bed.

'I always knew you were going to leave me,' my girlfriend said.

I pressed my tits together for the camera. Maybe she was saying it for me.

'You ever gonna tell me, Yara, what you really want?'

'I'm chicken,' I whispered, smiling uncontrollably.

But I believed in levels and visions, just like she did. I believed in sex as healing. I thought about Saturn and rape. I was addicted to the hours that we lay around in her room. I heard Manny say he wanted to see more of my face. Maybe I was too drunk now to get on a plane.

'I love you,' said my girlfriend.

She was on top of me, slippery, at my neck all over again.

'Yara,' Manny said. 'Look up at the light.'

Cold turkey, I thought. Get on the plane.

I thought, five years of mind-fucking are just about to end. *I love you, I love you, I love you so much.*

I was going to Israel tomorrow. I promised myself.

'That looks so good,' Manny said. 'Can I come in?'

In the periphery of my vision, I saw her face leak pain like sap.

I thought, if I'm an actress, I have to stop pretending right now.

✦

The lights dimmed in the classroom. A screen descended from on high. An actress appeared on it in close-up with a rust-tinted hairdo. Her voice sounded like a teacher's. 'Sluts,' she said with a lick.

My mother hated the word *slut*. She said her mother had called her that.

The woman onscreen with the beehive lay on a floating blue floor. She had on a tight black maid's skirt and a moulded cone-shaped bra. She was surrounded by women, one with a moustache. The professor stood near the door with a remote control, facing us. Tal said she'd had Mishi Berg her first year. Mishi was a sex-positive performance artist, infamous in the school. The actress held what looked like a mini-vacuum cleaner that she called her magic wand. All the women around her poked her sides while she masturbated with it. A counter timed ten minutes. My heart thumped in my throat.

I glanced at Tal quickly. She was writing in her notebook.

My grandmother once said to me, Your mother didn't have to run away. She said, I didn't always agree with her decisions, but she didn't need to leave.

'Every orgasm is a pattern,' the actress narrated in a baby-doll voice, 'a pattern of valleys and peaks.'

I wished that my mother and my grandmother got along. The group of women onscreen kept stroking and egging the maid on. Her vacuum vibrator droned. The woman started to come. Sticky, wet groans rolled low out of her throat. I heard someone laugh. I stared at Mishi Berg at the door. Suddenly, the groans got high-pitched, like the woman was being hurt. Onscreen, they didn't care. Everyone started to cheer. The digital clock sped. It showed us eight minutes had passed. The actress was shrieking, motor running, she was louder than the wand. For some reason, I remembered Aloni's oiled shoulders. Rabbi Fishman's black soles. As the lights in the classroom came on, I was breathing too fast. Everyone in the class clapped. I looked at Tal, but she didn't look back.

Mishi Berg stood behind a podium in the centre of the room. On the chalkboard behind her it said: Gender Studies 201.

'What was the crux of this video?' she asked.

Tal slid me a notebook. 'Yara, I got this for you.'

It was a black notebook with a gel pen in the spiral, exactly like hers.

Tal put up her hand before I could say thanks.

Mishi Berg stepped out from behind the podium. I held the notebook in my lap.

'Annie Sprinkle was a porn star,' Tal said confidently. 'So, this film was her first attempt to take things into her own hands.'

'Why do you think, Tal, that this was Sprinkle's first try?'

'Because the rest of her porn is woman-hating?'

'I consider "woman-hating" a stretch,' Mishi Berg said.

Tal got red in the face and started writing again.

'We just saw a woman have a really long cum,' some guy said. 'I don't understand the misogyny charge.'

'Because it sounded like she was being tortured.'

'Yeah, who breathes that fast?'

'Someone who's giving birth.'

'The screaming was disturbing.'

'Like a real horror flick.'

'Oh my God, shut the fuck up,' Tal said to herself.

I thought Mishi Berg was looking at me.

Define *slut*, I wanted to say. Berg, I know that you can't.

You can make one thousand U.S. dollars a month, my girlfriend had said.

'I would argue that Sprinkle on her back in the throes of uncontrollable pleasure is occupying a position of authority,' Mishi Berg said.

Oh wow, I liked that. *Authority* with legs spread.

You love sex, my girlfriend told me. It's your religion, Yara.

No one is going to gallop in on a horse to save you, my mother said.

Tell me you love me, said my girlfriend. Tell me at least once a day.

Go to your grandmother's, my mother yelled. I can't deal with you!

'And if we consider the tightly controlled contemporary Western construction of female sexuality,' Mishi Berg went on, 'perhaps we can understand Sprinkle in this video as an *aberration*.'

Authority. Aberration. Lists of new words like bullets.

'Because once female sexuality is no longer controllable, it is uncontrollable. And I believe that Annie Sprinkle here challenges our unspoken cultural rule that being fucked equals powerlessness.'

Tal leaned in to me. 'Yara, you should say something.'

'I want you all to write a personal reflection on Annie Sprinkle's *Sluts and Goddesses Video Workshop*, thinking about the notion of expanding the sexual and cultural role of women in the polis.'

People were packing up their knapsacks and leaving the classroom in groups.

I wrote in my new notebook: *Slut spread on her back like a king.*

'I want you to meet Mishi. She's amazing, isn't she?'

I held the notebook Tal gave me and followed her down the middle steps.

I was thinking about my mother. I was thinking about *authority* and *slut*. For the first time in my life, I considered not taking my grandmother's side.

'Dr. Berg, my friend Yara is here from Brazil. She wants to audit your class.'

Mishi Berg smiled. 'Welcome, Yara. What did you think?'

I thought, men all over the world have held my grainy pussy in their hands.

I heard Aloni asking what was inside our piggybank heads.

Mishi and Tal looked at me, waiting for me to speak.

'I think this stuff works on your mind,' I finally got out.

'What does?'

'Making pornography.'

Tal laughed. 'We got in trouble in Israel.'

'In trouble for what?' Mishi asked.

'Piggybanks,' I said quickly. 'Powerlessness.'

Mishi Berg looked back and forth between us. 'I'm not sure I understand.'

It felt like a layer of steak fat was lodged in my throat. Suddenly, I felt lucid. I wanted to organize myself. I mean, I wanted to organize my thinking. Make my thoughts real.

Anyone can learn how to write, Tal had said.

'Feel free to call me, Yara, if you'd like to talk about a course of study here. We have the best feminist film program in Canada, bar none.'

My grandmother was old-fashioned. My mother broke rank and file. My face ripped open like paper. I had words everywhere.

'Mishi loved you,' Tal said in the hallway. 'I could totally tell.'

What I gleaned from gender studies: cunt blocked can't speak.

I think I was translating something. I could be an actress. Like my girlfriend had said: everyone wants to see you have sex. My heart started skipping, free-sliding, maybe that's where I should be. Like the rust-tinted woman: in pornography.

✦

I was sleeping in a rich house with my own private toilet and sink. I'd been invited into this home like a refugee. One morning, when Tal was at the allergist with her mom, I went to Alan's office for a consultation.

His office was on the main street, a ten-minute walk from their house, over a storefront called Zimmer's Photographs. In the picture window, an oversized family photo of some kid's bar mitzvah hung from wires in mid-air. The background seemed golden, with faux spray-painted clouds. The kid wore a navy-blue suit with a baby-blue-and-white-striped tie. He was surrounded by busty sisters and his coiffed mom and dad. Upstairs, Alan's office was chaotic and cramped. It was full of rusted filing cabinets and craggy, long-faced African masks.

'Welcome, Yara,' Alan called from behind a massive mahogany desk. 'Come in. Don't be scared. Would you like a cappuccino? A bag of peanuts?'

I knew that Tal wanted me to stay in Toronto. She wanted us to study with Mishi, make feminist films. But on her brother's computer, I'd looked up the price of California motels. I'd looked up model agencies for girls who wanted to get into porn. I'd read on Yahoo that you didn't have to do anal. You could start easy, start slow.

Feminist, the word. I had it on me like a coat.

I watched Alan pour a plastic bottle of water into a coffee machine on an antique chest of drawers. It reminded me of the furniture in the photos of my grandmother's family.

'My daughter says you want to investigate your past with this woman and file a charge.'

There were stuffed pink file folders stacked on every surface in this room. I was thinking of porn as a landscape already inside of me.

'I'm not sure yet,' I said.

'It's not rocket science, kid.'

Tal had begged me to just listen to what he had to say. The coffee machine started to hiss. Alan patted it and slid a paper cup under a tube.

'So, it's easy. We record your deposition. Then we summon her to court.'

'A deposition?'

'The document, officially speaking, for us to use in the court. Oral sworn testimony. In English: your story, written down.'

Alan pressed another button and slid his coffee cup to the right. Milk bubbled out, soon overflowing the rim. My girlfriend had turned thirty and I'd been totally silent.

'Deposition is our preparation for the eventual judge. It's a precursor to her subpoena. It will be crucial for your charge.'

I was finally living without her. My own life, guilt-free.

'Yara, you on board?'

'Who does that?'

'Does what?'

'Records me,' I said.

Alan set the coffee down in front of me and sat behind his mahogany desk. 'A nice cappuccino. Let me serve you, my friend.'

A dirty window behind him separated the sky into squares. I realized that I hadn't thought about my girlfriend for two days. In Alan's clogged room, I saw her on a dark path. Running through Mindu's rubber leaves in spandex. *The eventual judge.* I smelled her cigarettes. I knew in a flash how my tongue loved her flesh.

'Let's be frank in here. My daughter told me that you wanted at the very least to challenge the woman who molested you. Am I correct on this, yes?'

'Molested?'

'That's what we say for young subjects. It gives emphasis.'

'It's not true,' I said, squeezing the paper cup. Foam sloshed on my lap.

'Settle down, Yara. We don't have to use it, I'm good to not use that word.'

Tal had convinced me to keep this meeting with her dad. But at Alan's office, I realized that I could not pinpoint what my girlfriend had actually done wrong.

'Do you need a serviette?'

Molestation? Fuck off. *Oy vavoy.*

'We know a lot of victims feel guilty, Yara. Especially when there was love.'

My mother told me that my girlfriend had set up camp outside our place. She was with some guy, my mother said, on the patch of grass in our driveway. According to my mother, the man started filming in a circle while my girlfriend danced on her knees. That woman is crazy, my mother warned. You need to keep staying away.

'Yara?'

I wiped my legs of spilled foam. I wanted to stop this process.

'Yara, we want your co-operation. A deposition is the first step. It will help you stay in Canada. You can be here as long as you want.'

He didn't know my plan. *Alan* and *anal* were not far apart.

'What would happen when she reads it?' I asked. 'My story, written down.'

'Very good question, Yara. But it's not so direct. This deposition is for us. She'd need a lawyer to respond. Then we subpoena. We subpoena her to trial.'

I saw myself like a fool beside Alan in a courtroom in Manaus. My mother behind me. My grandmother, face drawn. I knew it would never happen. I could not do that to her. My girlfriend was regal, mystical. Not a molester to charge.

'What if she ignores what we send her?' My voice sounded gruff.

'Kid, you can't ignore a subpoena.'

'You don't know her,' I said.

She would totally freak out. I knew my girlfriend would come after me wherever I was. My mother said she'd called the super, who told my girlfriend and Manny to leave. My mother said that if they ever came back, she would call the police.

Alan reached for the squished cappuccino that I hadn't drunk. 'If she ignores the court order, it could delay the procedure a bit,' he said. 'But then all we do is just send it again. We send it again until she knows the court is not kidding around. You can't ignore a subpoena because eventually cops knock on your door.'

I saw police outside her apartment, all their guns drawn. Dogs on the muddy slope, running in circles, tongues out.

'And then?'

'She is forced to make a statement, kind of like a reply. She'll get a lawyer who will contact me. Then we create a statement in response. We go back and forth with statements for a while.'

'Then what?'

'It goes to court if we cannot come to an agreement agreeably. I mean, once there has been an adequate back-and-forth.'

'What is an "adequate back-and-forth"?'

Alan slurped my cappuccino. 'It's not so cut and dried. It's more like a waiting game. We can call them to trial if they want the game to go on.'

'In Manaus, you mean?'

'Yes, that is where the crime took place.'

Crime. A fucking courtroom. My mouth bloomed with rank taste. Tal told me that her father charged five hundred dollars an hour.

'I don't want to do it.'

'Sexual exploitation has no jurisdiction, Yara. If you're uncomfortable, we can arrange to bring her over here.'

'No.'

'You don't want to do it at home and you don't want to do it here?'

'Right. That's right.'

'Okay, one step at a time, kid. I think you'll get there.'

Alan crumpled up the paper coffee cup and wiped his mouth with his hand. 'I think our best chance is to apply for arraignment over there. Let Joanna do the research.'

'Joanna?'

'My assistant. She's been to Rio. Carnaval.'

'I don't want to do this,' I said, standing up, ready to leave.

'Your mother disagrees.'

'My mother?'

Alan laughed. 'Yes, kid. Sit down. We've spoken with her. I mean, me and Gabby.'

'When?'

'Sit down, Yara. Your mother's very nice. She said that me and my wife could visit her in Brazil and she'd show us around.'

I didn't know what I was thinking, why I ever thought I could go to school and stay here. I felt violent, so violent, like I did in Israel. I should've stabbed Aloni, punched Joel, sucked Jonah to his death. Inside Alan's office, I felt my death mask.

'In your country, Yara, this stuff is all police-based. The feds rule the civil and none of them want to escalate. Police are not lawmakers. We don't do it like that here. And even with a case as serious as yours – I mean, underage, molestation – whatever we want to call it, there's not a lot of precedence for the domestic making it to court. If I wasn't involved, this would get tangled up in some godforsaken, municipal file … '

'I told you I was not molested, Dershowitz.'

Alan smirked. 'Trickster, eh?'

Trickster. Feminist. Actress.

'Look, Yara, I'll tell you the truth. I don't know what I'd do if this happened to my own kid.'

My heart felt like a fist. I wanted to show it to the world.

'I have the video,' I said.

Manny had sent me our first sex tape. He knew how to find it and attach it correctly, compressed.

'Oy,' Alan said. He was suddenly writing double-speed on his big yellow pad. 'Evidence accompanies deposition. Evidence pushes directly to trial. Asking for damages from the accused and the state.'

I was at Josh's computer. I saw her cat run in and out. Onscreen, I was crying. It was weird how young I looked. I was in Manny's eye. I was so clearly drunk. I covered my face. Naked and jellied and strange. My girlfriend tried to calm me down, squeezing my arm, stroking my hair. But my crying got worse. She had to restrain me with her weight. I was slapping her off me. Sex tape. I'd blocked that part out.

'Yara, in this case we sue for damages.'

Maybe I was crazy. Maybe I was being attacked.

I'm sorry, Yara, Manny wrote me.

'If she can't afford what we want, the state will come in.'

'No,' I said, shaking. 'I don't want her to know.'

'Sha, Yara. Impossible. Right now, you have to think of yourself.'

I thought, *yourself* was a puddle of mud. It was being unseen.

You two were in love, Manny wrote. *It was a whole other time.*

'Cut her out of your mind,' Alan said.

I felt jellied and schizoid. I'd drunk too much in that sex tape. My gut was muddy and shallow.

'You can stop this from happening to someone else,' Alan said.

✦

The last year we were together, my girlfriend said she didn't want to be a nurse. She said that being an assistant at the clinic was dulling her mind. She took me to her group that met every month at a one-room Pentecostal church. My girlfriend was getting into Umbanda. She said she mostly liked the music; it was going to help her transition to being a DJ.

At the church we sat on the wood benches, painted baby pink. We listened to a bubbly-looking woman in a white turban and layered white skirts.

'Possession is an honour from the ancestors,' she said. 'Possession is an honourable thing.'

In the pews were mostly older women and a few teenaged boys. The women wore African fabrics, caftans like you got at the market near her. Me and my girlfriend in our jean shorts stood out.

'One day, my sisters, we are going to talk without words. We will predict each other's thoughts. We will all be talking to each other with our eyes.'

My girlfriend glanced at me and I stared back at her. I quick-flickered my eyelids, making a joke.

'Umbanda is the music to call gods unseen. We must listen to the spirits in our bloodlines.'

At that point, with my girlfriend, I didn't understand the need to know about ancestors or 'generations past.' Like, I would never have wanted to be possessed by my great-grandmother. Why did people want to be ruled by their so-called bloodlines?

'This is dumb,' I whispered to my girlfriend.

She pinched my bare thigh. A flat-faced, brown-skinned Jesus had been painted on the wall.

Would I be a nightmare to my great-grandmother, a disappointment, or a curiosity? Or would her spirit stick to me irrepressibly?

We watched the women play drums as a few teenaged boys danced around them with arms in the air. There was a lot of chanting that I didn't understand.

After the drum circle, my girlfriend led me up to the white-robed priestess. She had green eyes that seemed lit from behind. She was a lot older than I'd thought, at least my grandmother's age. Her wrinkles were flat C-shaped seams in her face.

'This is Yara,' my girlfriend said to the priestess, bowing her head.

'Now I understand.' The woman nodded at me.

Then she put her hand on my arm. I felt a warm, thudding flood down through my wrist. My girlfriend squeezed my other hand so hard that my knuckles collapsed. It felt like five minutes, with the three of us like that, me in the middle of them. I felt some wonky flow coming through me of priestess heat.

When she suddenly released me, my girlfriend fell to her knees.

'Thank you, Mae-de-Santo!' she cried, head to the ground.

Eventually, everyone from the church was herded behind the dais. I was swept up in their feeling even though I felt weird. Women drank rum in shiny red glasses in the backroom of the church. The dancing teenaged boys passed around plates of peanuts and sweets.

My girlfriend looped her arm around my shoulder. 'We can be out here,' she said.

Music got piped in from the speakers and my girlfriend twirled me around. The women surrounded us, clapping. I felt peanuts hit my head. Mae-de-Santo started singing. Her stern, warbly voice filled my ears. I started laughing, twirling with my girlfriend, coins and peanuts at our feet. Everything felt exaggerated, vibrating, even the walls of the church. We pushed against each other. It was the most public we had ever been. Their voices were all singing something about moon flowers, flowers of the night. The women rang bells. The cave blurred with paint. My girlfriend pushed so hard into me I felt her clitoris pulse.

✦

Gabby took me out to her favourite restaurant, a downtown hotel's thirtieth floor. The place was filled with women lunching in poofy blouses and heels. The cutlery tinkled. Gabby ordered a bottle of Sancerre.

I felt ambushed by Tal's parents, both of them in their own way. Tal had presented me as someone who needed their authority.

'What is your mother like, Yara?' Gabby asked.

'My mom is cool,' I said quickly.

Gabby nodded like a robot. I smelled her magnolia perfume.

'You know, Yara, most children can't imagine that their mothers have lives.'

Gabby laughed nervously. My mother used to take me to her office if I didn't have school. That place was wood-panelled. It smelled like mothballs.

'I mean, I think most children want to imagine their mothers as perfectly equal to them. Of course, I had to tell

Tal when she was seven years old: Listen to me, kidlet. I know more than you. Of course, I realized, a little too late in the game, that Tal had to know I was in charge. Especially as a stay-at-home mom, which I don't know how I ended up being. Your mother sounds so much smarter than that, Yara.'

I wasn't going to tell Gabby that I lived with my grandmother for three years. When I started grade school, I was shuttled back to Manaus to live with my mom. I remember her boss as an old man with grizzly white hair and a paunch. My mother served him coffee and went out for dinners a lot.

'I had to be the alpha with Tal, not so much with Josh. Tal used to hit me, you know. She used to scratch and punch.'

'Really?' I said, laughing. I could not imagine that.

Gabby's face fell. 'Yes. I had bite marks and scratches halfway across my face. Alan did not believe either that his precious little girl could do that.'

I drank Gabby's fancy white wine thirty floors up from the ground. Surrounded by women and chandeliers, waiting for her theory of victimhood.

'More wine?' Gabby asked. 'And would you like a little nibble, Yara? They do a beautiful warm mushroom salad here. It's wild.'

I slid Gabby my glass. As I'd told her daughter and husband, I didn't really think I was damaged by having sex young. I liked warm mushroom salads, rich ladies, and lunch.

'You know, this is a bit roundabout, okay, but I'll start with this: I used to volunteer in Tal's lunchroom from kindergarten through Grade 6 … Do not volunteer in the lunchroom, Yara, when you have kids.'

Gabby drank her wine like water. She used it against me when she could not stop crying.

'When Tal was in Grade 3, maybe 4, I met this woman at the school who was also volunteering in the lunchroom. Or maybe she wasn't, I don't remember, it's all a blur. Her children were younger than Tal and she was telling me, in the lunchroom – I mean, the kitchen – I was stirring a big pot of soup. This was an alternative school, Yara – do you have those kinds in Brazil?'

In my girlfriend's estimation, I'd been a cruel and absent mommy who let her keep crying, who didn't know how to soothe.

'So, this woman, in the lunchroom, told me that she showed her kids her pads!'

Gabby leaned toward me, opening both her hands, as if showing me the horror of blood. A server came over and asked us if we were okay. Gabby winked at the woman and ordered another bottle of wine.

'Her bloody pads,' Gabby whispered. 'Do you believe that?'

I didn't know what to think about this misdirection. I was waiting for her expert's take about escaping sexual exploitation.

'Yara, are you understanding me? She showed her kids her period!'

Yes, I understood. 'Maybe she was just teaching them about how babies are made.'

'Oh,' Gabby laughed, covering her mouth. 'Oh no. She invited her kids into the bathroom with her!'

'I don't know. It really doesn't sound like such a big deal to me.'

Gabby suddenly went red like Talia, all up her neck to her cheeks. My mother walked around the apartment half-naked when she had a boyfriend. She didn't really care.

'Do you actually think that that mother was abusing her kids?' I asked.

'Oh my God. No, Yara. No. That's an exaggeration.'

Gabby waved at the waitress. More wine right now.

'I think it's problematic, that's all. I think that mother's boundaries were poor.'

I heard my mother having sex frequently. The first time I heard it, I guess I felt afraid but I was so young that I just told her the truth. My mother said, Our bodies are meant to have pleasure. We are meant to vocalize that. My mother told me that I'd have sex one day, too.

'I mean, her kids existed because of her period,' I said. 'Maybe that's all she told them. Maybe that's what she meant.'

Gabby sucked in air quickly and shut her mouth tight.

My mother was kind of hypocritical about sex. She didn't want me to have sex with my older girlfriend.

'I don't know why people think blood is so grisly,' I said, feeling the wine. 'It's only grisly if girls stab a pregnant woman and steal its living fetus, I think.'

Gabby covered her mouth, nauseated. She looked confused. The whole room tinkled with female teaspoons. A rainbow pierced my wine cup.

'Yara,' Gabby said, staring at me sternly, 'have you heard about the cycle of abuse?'

Right then our warm mushroom salad and another sweating bottle of Sancerre arrived. Gabby waited until the waitress uncorked it and poured us more wine.

'I'd like to hear your definition,' I said, drunk on mom-juice. The smell of the fungus invaded my nose.

'I define the cycle as being *fucked over*,' Gabby said. 'It's the ubiquity of being *fucked over* by someone who has been *fucked over* themselves.'

Gabby giggled a little. This is the reason Tal had brought me home.

'Like a snake eating its tail,' I said, smiling. 'Like a girl being restrained.'

'No, not like that,' Gabby said. 'Yara, listen to me. You shove something down and then you shove it down again. There is no nourishment. No freedom. No twitching. It's a pattern of burying. And it's intergenerational.'

Gabby drank more. I watched her. I buried myself in the sex tape? My mother was buried by my grandmother? Who buried Sharon Tate?

'Listen, we are knitting one line over and over again and we can't make a mitten or a sweater or even a patch. All this fretting, our trauma, Yara, doesn't turn into something. The knot is there. The lines are drawn. But we've made nothing.'

Gabby looked at her hands, interlacing them around her wine stem.

'Trauma makes you stuck. It's not productive, okay?'

I didn't want to swallow or be scolded. I was drunk. I felt fine.

'Everything is something,' I said. 'Every half mitten, half thought.'

Gabby shook her head sadly and topped up my glass. 'You know, Tal was very upset in Israel.'

Upset by my story? Upset with herself? I sloshed more wine down my hatch, burying words. Rich ladies, I thought, snorted wild mushrooms. Rich ladies had earlobes like testicles pierced with gold hoops. Mothers are dangerous, I thought. And their daughters are, too.

'Trauma catches up to you, Yara. Maybe you just don't know that yet.'

'I know it,' I said. 'I'm just doing something with it.'

I stood up from our table. I had my own way: fucked over, *productive*, through every hemisphere.

✦

I read Tal's script drunk, Sancerre in my veins. I had to look up a few words, like *psychosomatic*. Ha ha. Her story opened with a concept: a repeating problem of emotional abuse. It was in every generation of one family, as far back as 1900. There was always a mother and a daughter being photographed. It wasn't clear who was doing the abusing, or the photographing, or what the story was about. Anyway, after those first pages, it became the story of a family in the present day. There was a mother with a secret that impacted her kids. There was a brother and a sister, sixteen and nineteen. I felt like now I knew the secret. I recognized the bunker I was in.

The scene I liked best happened around page twenty-five. The sixteen-year-old girl was in her mother's closet trying on dresses that she loved. She stared at herself in an off-the-shoulder, flouncy white sundress cinched at the waist. Then she went to her friend's basement to have sex. The scene was mostly about the way the daughter looked at herself and felt in her mom's dress. She was described in the script as 'different than her mother, but with a manner the same.'

There were all these cameras in the story that related to the opening's photographs. When the daughter had sex with her friend in his basement, she kept her mother's dress on.

Actor-dependent, Tal wrote in the margins of the script.

I'd shown Tal the sex tape, the one Manny had sent.

Psychosomatic meant that your bodily problems were lodged in your mind.

Tal started crying when she saw me naked and drunk at sixteen. I wanted to tell her: *scapegoat* meant your intelligence roams up and down the hump of your spine.

Tal's script wasn't good. She didn't even describe what the mother looked like or how her daughter was different and the same.

I took a break at page forty. It was nine o'clock at night in Manaus. I slithered over to the computer. The computer was close to the bed.

I didn't want to write to my girlfriend, I really did not.

Tal begged me to let her father see the sex tape.

'It is the root of the abuse. It shows everything,' she said.

I'd had almost five full days without writing or feeling guilty about cutting her off. I'd actually felt stronger since sharing that image of me in the tape. I think because Tal felt for me, I felt something for myself.

How was your birthday, I typed into the chat.

I wasn't thinking about the law. I thought I would just quickly log in and log out. Sancerre, trauma-talk, I licked my lips, felt alive. I sat at Josh's slab of plywood, kind of proud of myself. I felt like I could talk to her without lying. I actually felt this kind of hope for my future for the very first time. I wanted her to know me like this: independent.

How was my birthday? my girlfriend finally typed back.

You're there! How did it go? I hope it was good!

We didn't sell enough tickets to rent the place, Yara.

She was selling tickets to her birthday? I didn't know that.

I thought that night was going to change my whole life.

I knew my girlfriend had been planning this party as her DJ debut.

You didn't come home. It was ruined.

She was blaming me for the party not going through?

My family won't talk to me. I am totally alone. You have no fucking idea, you have no fucking clue how that feels.

It wasn't my fault that her party was cancelled. That made no sense.

You don't care about me, Yara. After everything we've been through. Sometimes I don't want to live. But you don't want to hear about that.

I felt like my girlfriend was choking me from her couch in Manaus.

Tal kept on telling me that her father understood everything.

Will you try again? I typed quickly. *I mean, to DJ somewhere else.*

Yara, I am fucking thirty years old!

I thought about us dancing in the Pentecostal church. I thought about the good things, not her lashing out.

I am telling you I thought that night would change my life. You're changing the subject. I'm not fucking crazy. I have a reason to be upset!

What subject? I typed.

Christ, I don't feel like explaining myself all over again! You know. Don't lie. You know what I'm talking about.

I knew that being a DJ was going to be a problem in her life just like everything else.

Tal had convinced me to show her dad the sex tape.

I wanted to pull the plug on the computer. I wanted someone to believe my side, how I felt.

I imagined you with me, you and me TOGETHER, Yara. Do I have to spell that out? I imagined us together on my birthday. I imagined you would finally say yes to our life.

I was conscious of blinking. I wanted to keep my eyes closed.

Can Manny help you? I typed.

Fuck you, Yara.

Her hatred emanated. A deft, choking operation.

Right after I wrote about Manny helping her, I knew it was the wrong thing to say. But he was always there to be with her, no matter how hopeless she got. I guess I really didn't know how to articulate my care. But I just had my own feelings that were different than hers. I had no other experience. I didn't know how love worked. All I knew then: manipulation was not it.

You really don't know how lucky you are, do you?

That's what Joel said in Israel. You won the lottery, Yara.

You don't know what it is to grow up without anyone caring about you. You don't know what it's like to have a family who thinks you're insane. You run on luck, Yara. People think you're innocent.

Tal's house was too big. I knew I'd drunk too much wine. I didn't win the lottery and I wasn't innocent.

I pray every night. I made protection for you.

I held on to Josh's desk. I felt the heat of the hard drive between my two thighs. I knew she didn't know I'd emailed Manny, that I'd asked him for the sex tape. It was evidence. Incontrovertible. She'd want to kill me, I thought.

You've got the kind of life, typed my girlfriend, *where people just give things to you.*

Saliva dripped in a trickle off the cliff of my throat.

Things will get better, I wrote quickly. *I know that, I do.*

You're a liar, Yara. Nothing will ever fucking change in my life.

I saw her crying. I knew the incense was lit. She was punching things, burning things, hurting herself.

When are you coming back? she typed. *Tell me the date.*

Once, she seared her thigh with a cigarette.

You have no idea what it is to go to a job every day somewhere you hate.

I hated our fighting. I hated the feeling of not being able to escape.

You can get a different job, I typed, desperate. *You can work somewhere else.*

Do you not fucking understand that my family could starve?

I'm sorry, I typed for the one thousandth time.

Sorry for what? What are you sorry for? Sorry for leaving here without me?

I stared cross-eyed at my hands near the computer's keys.

You think you're too good for me, Yara. But you're fucking not. You think I'm jealous of you, don't you?

Should I type: I don't think that?

You're not as smart as you think you are, Yara. And you're not as hot as you think you are, either.

I braced myself. I saw myself. I heard Tal crying for me.

Have some fucking empathy, Yara. Can't you see I'm in pain?

She wanted me down. She wanted me hopeless like her.

I have to go now, I typed as calmly as I could.

Yeah, run away. Go. You're a coward. Self-professed.

I thought of that chicken in her parents' backyard kicked in the beak. I was lying. I was sweating. I was done with all this. I remembered how my girlfriend used to say that we were kin. I realized right then and I never wanted to forget: if my girlfriend was drowning, she'd take me under with her.

One day, you're going to know what it feels like for me. One day, you'll regret this. One day, you'll see.

I kicked Josh's hard drive until it cut out.

In that tape, it occurred to me, I had not been fully conscious.

I told Tal that she could show it to her father to help.

I had to rise from the murk like a monster, wings dripping slick.

My new name was *Dershowitz, Dissenter, Brazzers, Brasilia.*

✦

In Israel, Tal had told me that her mother was a survivor of sexual abuse.

'Inappropriate touch' is what Gabby said at the end of our second bottle of Sancerre.

'He was drying her after the shower,' Gabby said, twirling her hair. 'He had the towel behind Tal, opened up like a cape.'

Her eyes widened and she shivered. She looked like a mare.

'Alan ran upstairs and got my father to stop whatever he was doing. Of course, it was just playing. He didn't do anything. Tal barely even remembers. Yara, all this wine … '

I was confused. Was the survivor of sexual abuse Gabby or Tal?

'I thank God every day that there was no harm done. What happened to Tal is not what happened in my childhood.'

It felt like she had been thinking about those sentences, in that order. It sounded rehearsed.

'Tal was laughing and happy when Alan got upstairs. Alan just told my father to come back down for dessert. It was nothing. Nothing happened. I'm sure about that.'

Sancerre was vapour, acrid, candy-like.

'Tal doesn't even remember,' Gabby repeated. 'I never wanted to ruin her impression of him. My father was a good man. He didn't do anything.'

I didn't want to tell her: I think you are wrong.

'Why are you looking at me like that, Yara? Have I said something bad?'

'Tal remembers,' I said. 'I know that she does. You've told her the story of your sexual abuse survivorhood.'

Gabby coughed. She looked green. 'Maybe I have.'

I put her denial together for her: what happened to Gabby was almost replicated in Tal.

Gabby's mouth sagged with a goofy, sad grin. She was bunged up, digging holes. She couldn't talk about this.

I couldn't believe Tal had pitched her mother to me as the epitome of health.

I remembered my girlfriend like taffy, taffy between fingertips.

Then Gabby covered her face and sobbed on the tablecloth.

I put my hand on her head and said *shhhh*.

When Gabby finally sat up, she looked at me anew. The cutlery stopped tinkling. The chandeliers dimmed.

'I feel much better,' she said, red-eyed, motioning for the bill.

I thought, this is what kind of mother I'd one day become: a mother who tries to stop things from re-happening in the cycle of victimhood.

✦

I bought the plane ticket to California with my grandmother's cash. I booked a motel in Van Nuys on Victory Boulevard called the Starlight. I packed the notebook Tal got me, filled with my new words. I was going to tell her I was leaving after the second meeting she'd scheduled with me and her dad.

'He wants to help you,' Tal kept saying. 'He wants to get you justice.'

I didn't want to tell Tal that he was imagining her as the one crying, being drunk and restrained.

Outside, in the backyard, Alan lit torches in a circle round us. The recliners had long white-and-navy-striped pillows like we were on a ship.

'The office felt too official, right, girls?'

Tal handed me a glass of red wine. The torch lights looked like goldfish. The air was humid and floral.

'Justice is a process,' Alan said.

I'd collected a list of agencies for models, a chunk from my grandmother in USD. The tape recorder sat on a patio table beside Alan's yellow legal pad. Their house like a bunker behind us was scaled with vines. Two crooked lilac trees stood out in the dark. It felt like a deer could run through this backyard.

I felt like I had experience with shooting sex. I knew that Tal wouldn't want me to go to California for this. But I thought of it as my pilgrimage, repairing a hole. I had this real vision of my sexuality needing to develop onscreen: girl-with-nose-job-learning-to-swallow-and-speak.

I wanted to implant my whole self in the frame with Josh Dee. I wanted to have sex and scream. I thought Josh Dee would cancel out my girlfriend. I'm not sure why I thought that.

'I used to be on the radio,' Alan said, sloshing his wine side to side in the glass. 'I've fought battles for justice for twenty-five years. Did Tal tell you about the time I took on Canada's energy syndicate?'

I stood up from my pillowed patio chair for more wine. I felt Alan's eyes follow my fringed belly tee that I bought on the Jamaican side of the street.

'That shirt looks really good on you,' Tal said.

'Thanks,' I said to Tal, curtseying.

I felt sexually exaggerated, already in flight.

'Yeah, so we are talking about matters of justice, Yara's case … '

Alan slid Tal his yellow legal pad. He turned on the tape recorder.

'Are we ready?' he asked.

I nodded and stayed standing, thinking about my girlfriend.

'We always start in a deposition with what harms were incurred,' Alan said, 'and we know that most sexual assault victims suffer a loss of dignity. Can you tell us, Yara, how the accused made you feel?'

Tal looked up at me, her eyes reflecting the flame of the torch. I rolled my eyes without thinking. I wished she wasn't her dad's pawn.

I said, 'Loss of dignity is not a great place to start.'

'Excuse me,' Alan coughed. 'Of course, you are right. Sexual abuse victims may also suffer a variety of other consequential harms. Such as feelings of shame and self-blame, depression and suicidal thoughts. We've seen addictions, sleep disorders, sexual dysfunction, the whole lot.'

'Dad,' Tal interrupted. 'Let Yara speak.'

Tomorrow I'd call my mother from the airport and tell her where I was.

'The courts, especially in the backwaters – excuse my French,' Alan went on, 'are faced with the challenge of evaluating these so-called *intangibles*. These *intangible injuries* vary greatly depending on the nature of the victim.'

Suddenly, I felt distracted. *Intangible*. I looked for the deer.

'Yara, he's trying to help you. We need your help with this part.'

I drank my second glass of wine standing. I wanted a hoof to the nose.

'I think my nature is sluttiness,' I said.

Alan scratched his arm. 'Yara, this is not a joke.'

'*Slut*'s not a slur,' I said. 'And neither is *scapegoat*. Sex tapes, I believe, are the art of the scapegoat.'

'Stop,' Alan said. 'I don't know what you're talking about.'

Tal had a red neck. She stood up. She sat down. I saw her blowing out candles every year on big birthday cakes in this yard. I saw Gabby clapping, kids running through sprinklers, lilacs wild.

'Listen to me, Yara. We can stop and start fresh. What we have to expect is that the court in Manaus will assess general damage by considering the particular aggravating features of our case. Such as the number of assaults you endured over a period of time, the ages at which those assaults occurred, the frequency and duration of the abuse and the like … '

I started to pace. Assault, abuse. This wasn't right.

'Press Record,' Tal said.

'I was with her every single weekend from fifteen to twenty years old. On holidays we spent every day together, always at her place, in bed. We cooked and we had sex. What you are calling abuse … ' I stopped walking. 'I think my girl-friend just loved me too much.'

Tal wrote double time. I felt wind through my nose.

'Coercion, emotional abuse, primes the victim for all degrees of suffering,' Alan said, looking up at me. 'Did you feel coerced into sex with her, Yara?'

Tal kept her head down.

The moon, way up high, slipped through the thin, char-coal clouds. I thought I should sit but I needed to stand.

'I didn't feel coerced. But she, uh, called me a lot. Some-times, ten times until I picked up. She stood outside of my school. I was embarrassed by that. She was a lot older than me. And, um, being a woman … I mean, none of my friends at school knew about that.'

'Yara, okay. Start at the beginning again.'

'I was fifteen and she was twenty-five when we met.'

'Good. Just the facts,' Alan said. 'Very simple. Like that.'

'She was my nurse in a clinic for cosmetic surgery. Did you know that almost every single woman in Brazil gets something done? It's a part of our culture. We have the most beautiful women in the world. Brazilians think cosmetic surgery is a kind of levelling. Beauty is a right that transcends class, everything. Did Tal even tell you I had a nose job?'

'Good to know, Yara,' Alan said. 'But you're veering off course.'

'Sometimes I think we're right about beauty and some-times I think we're wrong. Sometimes I think a nose job is violence: the violence of beautification.'

Alan nodded. 'Go on.'

'She was my nurse and we became friends.'

'Good. She did not recruit you or groom you, correct?'

'She saw me when I was under, if that's what you mean.'

'It's not, but I'm glad you are speaking your truth finally. My daughter said you were reluctant to go forward with this … '

'Dad.'

'Because we know it's best to strike while the iron is hot.'

'Strike what?'

'It's a saying.'

'What do we strike?'

'I mean, when the crime was not so long ago, that's when we go in.'

'She doesn't have money,' I said. 'She's not a real nurse.'

'As I told you, the defendant's financial situation is not our concern.'

Alan thought I was stalling. Tal kept her head down.

'Listen, Yara, this is good. We know you're a sensitive girl. But you just cannot worry about that woman anymore. She took advantage of you in a criminal capacity, filming you when you were underage. We have a term for that in this country: child pornography.'

God, that could not be the definition. I sat down. I refused to believe. They'd both seen the tape. I was not a child.

'Yara, listen to us. You need to worry about your own future now.'

'He can get gold from stones,' Tal said. 'Gold from anything.'

Money was not everything. It wasn't what I was looking for in pornography.

'Money will make things easier for you,' Tal said, as if reading my mind.

I can make money myself, I thought. I'm a grown-up. So are you, Tal.

'Okay, let's backtrack to where would you be if you had not had this relationship,' Alan said. 'The goal of our request is to put you back where you would have been.'

Child porn was not true. In my case, it was a trick of language.

'I'd be at home,' I said.

'At school? You mean, university?'

'She didn't want me to go.'

'Good. That's not good. Tal, write that down. Education is key, as we all know.'

'Gender studies does not exist in Manaus.'

'And your mental state, Yara? Would you be the same person if not for her?'

I'd never thought of that before. Who would I be? A true-crime girl, looking for gold in the sand? Gesticulating, like Dershowitz, with a red nose tip? If I hadn't met her at the clinic, when would I have had sex?

'We all know it is criminal to film a minor in an explicit fashion,' Alan said. 'But I think our best angle here is mental distress.'

'Maybe I'm destined to repeat the same things,' I said, suddenly smiling.

'Good! That's good, Yara. Can you elaborate on that?'

I stared at Tal, her head down in notes. I'd be the same person, I realized, with my girlfriend or without. I felt a sudden twitch in my body, a desire to dance. Sluttiness was not a crime. Neither was curiousness.

I said, 'All girls are needy. They're explorers. They need to cure their fear of demons.'

'Demons? Oy. Yara, please. Stick to the question. What can we can say about your repeated behaviours? Sleeplessness, crying jags, panic, weight gain?'

My girlfriend's silky fingers hooked in and out of my throat.

'I wish it hadn't happened,' I blurted. 'I wish I'd never met her.'

'Oh, Yara,' Tal said, putting down her pen.

Alan slid the recorder closer. 'So, tell us, who shot that terrible tape?'

'It is not child porn.'

'Semantics,' Alan said.

Tal's sorry sponge eyes drew down in shame.

'That was my daughter's question, Yara. She should've followed me into law.'

'Manny shot it,' I said.

I knew Tal knew that. I was the deer, bungling through silky black grass.

'Tal, write that down. Can we get him to make a statement? An appearance in court?'

'I have a statement,' I said, holding up my wineglass.

The old sprinkler flooded my vulva. It tickled up my spine.

'I'm going south to California.'

'No, you're not, Yara. Now is not the time.'

Tal kept her head down. I saw her pen poised.

'Oral sworn testimony,' I said. 'Write this down: I am the people's masturbation. I might as well make use of that.'

I was sort of joking, but Tal didn't laugh.

'I have not been abducted like Gilad Shalit.'

Alan turned off the recorder. 'We have enough,' he mumbled to himself.

I caught Tal's eyes. I tried to smile at her.

There were so many things I'd never said to my girl-friend out loud. The most important one: *I-don't-want-to-be-blamed-anymore.*

I knew I had no authority when Manny filmed me. But Manny had apologized. She never did.

✦

'Who here knows the real story of Judaism and Christianity?' Rabbi Fishman had asked us in Tzfat.

Joel piped up first: 'We roasted Jesus on a spit.'

Rabbi Fishman held up both his hands and everyone laughed.

'Taglit, you would not joke if we still had this mode of punishment. Crucifixion, you understand, used to take a whole week. You had blood running down you, pus and plasma and poop.'

'Gross,' Reena said.

'Then, after seven days, when all your leaking was done, maggots multiplied and crawled out of your nailed-down wounds.'

'Gross,' Reena said.

Tal had just hooked up with Etgar, a soldier, one of our Birthright guests. He had dusty skin, pea-soup pants, and a gun strapped at his side like a purse. Etgar told us what it was like to be called to the front lines. He said that for young kids like him, it made you terrorized. Not to use a weapon, he said, but to understand the mindset to fight. Etgar poked his temple. He said: We Jews understand hate.

'I know the story of Judaism and Christianity,' I said.

'Finally!' Fishman cried. 'A Birthright girl who knows this!'

Aloni was still proud of me then. I was his prize from Brazil.

Tal said that Etgar fucked girls from Birthright to get American experience. His cum tasted like onions. His cock, ringed with hair.

'On the road to Damascus, Paul hallucinated,' I said. 'Paul the Apostle, the first Christian, was really a Jew. I think he sort of fell in love with Jesus and wanted to tell everyone.'

Fishman clapped. Then he laughed.

I thought, it is easy to lose your mind in this land.

'So, what were the Jews supposed to do about the growing number of their brethren attracted to Paul's ways?' Fishman asked.

'They couldn't help themselves,' I said. 'They were pulled to him, too.'

Fishman's bare feet on the rotten floor mesmerized me.

'It's not widely known, Taglit, there was resistance to this.'

Rabbi Fishman paced the centre of the circle, looking at me. 'Around the year 100 of the Common Era,' he said, 'the rabbis instituted a formal ban on Paul's Jewish Nazarenes.

'But let's head backwards for a minute. What we know from our Brazilian friend is that on the road to Damascus, something happened to Paul. Unusual or mystical, hallucination, call it what you will. What happened was that Paul identified with Jesus. *His wounds are my wounds.* Blah-blah. You understand? *He died for my sins.* This was the problem, Taglit! This new way of thinking: *He died for me.* Like, think about a song, okay, inciting you to kill. It is an occurrence in Sweden, with heavy metal … '

Joel guffawed. Fishman stopped walking around.

'Identification is very dangerous,' Fishman said, stabbing his middle finger at me. 'One bad trip, one bad mirror, and your whole life will change.'

Then Fishman from Philadelphia circled his stabbing finger in the air.

'*I hurt just like the messiah.* This was Paul's revelation. My friends, this is the pre-eminent Christian teaching. It is the central rift between us and them. The difference between Judaism and Christianity is in the understanding of pain. They believe pain is transmissible. This, my Jewish friends, is a very dangerous thing to have to live.'

I stared at my hands and felt like I braced for a punch. It was like Fishman knew what had happened with my girlfriend for five years. I mean, how her pain became mine. How it zigzagged like a live wire, how it penetrated me.

'Around the year 100,' Rabbi Fishman went on, 'if you, as a Jew, believed like Paul that Jesus was Mashiach here to redeem all your sins, the rabbis said to their congregations: "You are no longer welcome to pray with us. Get out of our synagogues! Convert yourselves to them!"'

Tal put up her hand. I saw her mouth dripping with cum.

'But how did they know?' she asked. 'How did they know what you believed?'

Fishman from Philadelphia smiled beatifically.

'If someone suspected their fellow Jew of harbouring Christian beliefs, that person had to lead the blessings,' Fishman said. 'Lead the blessings, let's see. Okay, man, no problem, a lot of Jews thought. But when the suspect got to the blessing for heretics – the Birkat haMinim, that is actually a curse – and they skipped over it, that meant: I reject my Christian leanings; that is, I am a Jew. But if the suspect still read it, unaware, he would be ejected from the synagogue on his tuchus, just like that!'

'Bullshit,' Jonah whispered. 'This guy is a kook.'

No, he was right. This was the scapegoat's revelation!

My girlfriend always said she knew what I thought. She said we were connected, thought to thought, pulse to pulse. She said, Mother and baby survive together, not alone.

I was like Paul: blinded and then I could see.

I could not convert to her vision of love. I could not. It wasn't for me.

'Paul left Palestine on a voyage as far as China to spread this imagined, new way of seeing life and death,' Fishman said. 'Paul started talking and talking, now to pagans more than Jews. To people who were ready to hear that Jesus could bathe you in light.

'Share your pain. Tell it, Paul the wanderer said. Jesus died for your sins. Jesus loves you and you can be saved!'

I felt so dizzy in the synagogue of Tzfat.

I was emerging from the pain-is-love cocoon.

Fishman's teaching was revealing everything to me: identification is delusion. There is another way to be with human beings.

Fishman stalked our circle, grinning maniacally. 'Birthright, there is a very strange painting related to the story of Judaism and Christianity that I will tell you about. It comes from around the year 200 of our collective human history. The painting is of two women who appeared very differently. And if you were illiterate then, Taglit, as most of our brethren were, you would take in all the details of this image to suss out its meaning.'

Fishman looked right at me. I think he felt my trembling.

'The woman on the right, we see her standing in a beautiful draped dress. She looks to the horizon, holding a staff. The other woman that you see is slumped over, half-dressed drunk at her feet. She's wrinkled and drooling, riding a goat's head.

'Tell me, Taglit, what did these women represent?'

I put up my hand like a dart. I would finish this off.

'It meant that Christianity was the future,' I said.

Fishman nodded, gesticulating.

'And the slumped-over woman signified the carnal nature of Jewishness.'

Fishman clapped wildly, motioning us all to get up. 'Christians thought they could kill us, make us extinct. Break these bonds! Here we are! Dance, Birthright, dance!'

That's when we all did the hora, stomping around. 'Hava Nagila' piped in from above. Paul and Jesus, obsessively in love. A drunk, horny woman blamed for Judaism's demise.

'Dance, Birthright, dance! You are waiting for what?'

I started to laugh. I felt omnipotent.

Crime doesn't correspond to justice, I learned in Israel.

Justice needed a confession, Canada revealed.

I was a loping Jewish female, pain-free and California-bound.

I knew scapegoats shed their delusions to reach higher ground.

RIGHTBIRTH

I arrived in your country September 2006. *Porn*, the one word everyone understood.

'You checked off Work here,' said the agent. 'Work, not pleasure.'

My motel in Van Nuys was fifty-five dollars a night.

'Pleasure means *leisure*. It means you don't work.'

I shrugged at the man and tried to look cute.

'Okay. Let's try again, Miss Yavelberg. What are you doing in California today?'

Repelling plastic, gloved fingers almost exactly like hers.

The agent rescanned my passport and typed on a keyboard that beeped.

'You have a boyfriend, Miss Yavelberg? Who's picking you up?'

It felt like the agent was feeding me peanuts through bars.

'No boyfriend. Okay, where are you staying then?'

'Van Nuys,' I stated. 'Victory Boulevard.'

'Name of residence?'

'Where I'm staying?'

'Yes, your address.'

'Victory Boulevard,' I repeated. 'I'm visiting someone.'

'Okay, Miss Yavelberg, that's not how this works. Who are you seeing in California?'

The agent flipped through my passport stamped with Israel. I'd ticked Work on immigration because that would be the truth. I'd looked up shopping malls and supermarkets. I'd looked up PINK TV. I had a list of model agencies, a list of production companies.

'My friend from Birthright,' I said.

'What's her name?'

'Tal. Talia Ruben. She's here with her parents.'

'And then you're going back home to Brazil?'

'Yes.'

'Plane ticket, please.'

'I don't have it yet.'

The agent punched my passport. He looked at my sweet eyes.

'My grandmother's going to send it to me.'

'Lucky girl,' said the agent.

I won the lottery, I thought.

'Work or pleasure, Miss Yavelberg?'

'Pleasure,' I said.

He gave me back my passport. Pleasure was rightbirth.

✦

I was the only one walking on Sepulveda Boulevard. I wore the thick leather sandals I'd bought in Israel. My dress had a gauzy pink butterfly wrapped around the top. I was happy not to be a teenager anymore.

Teenage slut was the number one porn search on Yahoo. I strutted in my Israeli-made sandals with two forced pigtails. Girl alone, pantyless, butterflied tits. Were my inner and outer life so completely different? I mean, I wanted this costume to be nuanced – like, you think I'm one thing, but I'm not. Dumb and pigtailed: a woman with knowledge. Cars passed me, beeping. The sun cracked my lips. Palm trees towered above me like giant beanstocks. I wondered if I could keep up the facade of all this. Like, slut on the hunt – but innocent, she won't bite! The address I was looking for was in a strip mall. It was set far back from the road, cars parked on the diagonal.

The Naughty Nice agency looked like an old grocery store. There was no bell to ring, just a small sign on the door. The picture window in front was plastered with newspapers and tape. I didn't feel nervous but I smelled animal shit.

I knocked lightly. No one answered. The door was unlocked.

'Hello?' I said at the entrance.

Facade cracking. My voice came out weak.

Four guys sat in a circle on cheap folding chairs. Newspapers were taped on the floors, they seemed taped everywhere. The place was being painted, full of construction dust. Red wires hung from the ceiling. Stuffed boxes stacked against walls. I wasn't sure this was Naughty Nice or why they hadn't come to the door.

'You called us, I spoke with you. What's your name again?'

A guy in a saggy-necked T-shirt and white jeans stood in front of me.

'Yara. Yara Yavelberg.'

'We can change that,' a guy said from the circle of chairs.

My armpits prickled. My breasts felt bruised. The men back there seemed older, some with white hair. I concentrated on the one right in front of me. He seemed about thirty-five years old but he had cracked, greyish teeth.

'Excuse the mess. We just moved in. Can I get you something to drink?'

I couldn't help it. I thought, what if my girlfriend saw me in this room with these men?

'You're our very first girl,' the guy said. 'I'm Bryan. Follow me.'

We passed the circle of men toward the back. I felt bald, on an axis walking past them.

'She can pass for American,' someone said.

'If she doesn't speak.'

'I like them with accents.'

'I like her big tits.'

Bryan handed me a bottle of Diet Coke from a crate on the floor. The cap's rim had been broken. It was only half-full. I noticed a transistor radio splattered with gloop. Slut on the hunt. It's easy to look oversexed. I followed the guy down a dark hallway full of holes in the wall. He held a stuffed plastic bag. He opened a door.

'You can get changed in here. The pink set. Sorry, lights aren't working yet.'

In the bathroom there was a small dusty window, a mirror, weak sun coming through. Bryan closed the door. I didn't feel like a slut. I didn't feel innocent, either. I felt like a hole in the wall.

Inside the bag Bryan gave me was a bunch of lingerie. The pink set was a baby-doll teddy the colour of worms. A ruffle of fluorescent fake fur at the hem. The matching pink panties had a hole in the crotch. Oversex, undersex, inside and out. I was the needle. I was alone.

Tal had been upset I was leaving. She'd sat on my bed in Josh's room, watching me pack.

I don't think this is all just going to go away, Tal said.

I slid on the teddy. The material itched.

'You okay in there?' Bryan knocked.

I was going to go out like this.

In the Starlight, with pink razors, I'd shaved off all my hair.

Tal said, You can call me anytime, Yara. Night or day, you know that.

Bryan was right there outside when I opened the door.

'Shit,' he said, abruptly looking at my feet.

I was still wearing the Israeli sandals, buckled leather and flat. Bryan slid past me into the bathroom, apologizing. There was a shoe rack in one corner that I hadn't seen.

'Size?'

Bryan crouched down and measured my foot to his hand. He extracted a pair of high heels, pink vinyl and cracked.

'Okay?' he asked me, looking up my thighs.

I saw him glace at my vulva. My vulva felt bloated and strange.

I'd told Tal before I left that I wanted to stop the court case. She said her dad wouldn't stop working. The deposition had been sent. Tal said we had to finish things off. We had to do the right thing. I'd be protected, Tal said. Bryan unstrapped my left sandal. His hands were gummy and warm.

'I like feet, man, I can't help it,' he said, running two fingers under my arch.

I laughed without meaning to. I was ticklish.

Bryan slipped off my other sandal and slid my foot into the cracked, pink high heel.

'Nice,' he said. 'They fit good, Yavelberg.'

When he stood up, he was really close to me. He brushed by my fur hem.

'The guys think your name should be exotic, with your accent and all.' I was eye height with him in the heels.

Bryan's face was chiselled and boxer-like. He clamped his hand on my forearm and led me back down the hallway. I felt dust in the slit of the panties. I walked hip to hip.

'Here she is. Voila. Miss Yavelberg.'

Bryan didn't let go of my arm. The guys all pushed their chairs backwards, giving me space. Bryan stood with me in the middle and spun me around. One of the men stubbed a cigarette on a newspaper under his shoe.

'Very nice.'

'Double D?'

'I think C,' Bryan said.

'D or double. No way are those girls less than that.'

'Our vision is classy, does she understand?'

'Lingerie for a man and his wife. This is private ads only. You don't have to tell your parents, okay, Yavelberg?'

'I thought this was a film production company,' I said, on the verge of something.

Bryan looked embarrassed. I stared at him over the men's heads. Laughing or crying, I wasn't sure what. A bubble in my throat. A bubble for a face. I wanted to look sexy. I wanted to act.

'We got busted,' Bryan said. 'We had to relocate. Rebrand.'

The teddy had spaghetti straps. My breasts felt too heavy for that. My nipples both hurt, like pinpricks or something. My girlfriend always said my breasts were tasty sugar flesh. Cantaloupes. The underside. I loved her sucking on them.

'Tell her to do a little turn. Be girlish. Something.'

My performance was not working. These men didn't even make films! I was not cute with deep thoughts. I was no slut on the hunt. I heard Aloni in my head. Or maybe it was Alan.

'Nice bikini, Yara. But you need a new shtick.'

'We call this one the midnight nightie for sex time. Can we see the eye slit?'

My engorged little vulva. My engorged little brain.

'Is she gonna take it off?'

'We spoke about it,' Bryan said.

Bryan was setting up a tripod with a tiny camera on top. I thought about the way he'd massaged my feet in the john.

'Don't be scared, Yara, you are beautiful,' Bryan said.

But my skin felt all fractalled, like Tal's mottled hives.

'May I?' Bryan said, walking into the circle again.

Dazed Manson girl. Dunce-like. Gummy four limbs. Bryan's breath smelled like yogourt. I felt something bloom in the slit.

Bryan slid one big hand down the nightie's V-neck. He lifted my breast up into the cup with the seam. He surgically lifted the other. His hands felt as sure as they had with my feet.

'Nighties look better with nipples, darling.'

Then Bryan took my left nipple between his fingers and twisted it hard. My eyes watered. He didn't do the other. I didn't know why.

'Let's take a few pictures and see how we do.'

My jaw felt protruded. I had donkey teeth.

'You look a little hungry. Let's see the lips closed.'

I walked around the circle like cattle. I bit my lip shut. I had to make my right nipple be even bigger than the left. I heard the other guys breathing, old men all around. This was an introduction to the auction. I committed to it. I spiralled in the centre of the circle, heavy breasts and squished toes. I wanted them to see me from every angle. I licked my lip, felt my fur hem. Cracked heels, *feminist*, nipples like eyes. I heard multiple breaths. I thought, my girlfriend started this. She made everything sex. I don't know why it was addictive to be thought of like this. My girlfriend would hate me here. Same as Tal. This was their antithesis.

But I was the star in the centre of men. I was a sex star, fireworks shot through my head. *Naughty Nice. True crime. Brazzers-Brasilia.* What did it matter who was watching me, I thought. I had eyes on my body. I was looking back.

Dershowitz-Dissenter. All watching was the same. Bryan took pictures. The radio played. I was a sex star on the airplane. Sex star in the park. Sex star on Saturn, studded and ocular. It was working, I was moving, I was dancing to shake. *Malefic Brazzer*, get ready to fuck.

'Very nice,' said a guy.

'Naughty nice,' I said back.

All the guys laughed. I bent down, shimmied up.

'Show us the slit.'

I didn't hear a shutter click. It occurred to me that that camera made videos.

'She's a D, man.'

'We like the jiggle.'

'Let it go, girl.'

'I like you, Yavelberg.'

I squatted right down to the construction floor. I opened my thighs. My pussy hung down three feet. I could scrub things with it. Scrub the floor with my pussy. Make a big mess.

Was it all an act? wrote my girlfriend. *Yara, tell me the truth.*

No, I wrote back from the Starlight's cubicle.

I wrote her again even though I said I would not. I tried Tal at first but she didn't respond.

I moved from squat up to straight legs and from straight back to squat. Bryan looked at me squint-eyed. He lit a cigarette.

Yara, wrote my girlfriend, *you've been body-snatched.*

I had a nasty-nice monstrous body made of jelly and slits. I felt a hand on my leg, yanking the fur-rimmed hem from behind. The men's chairs had come closer. I was jiggling and twisting for them.

'Told you,' Bryan said. 'She's a natural, man.'

Crouch and fold, crouch and fold, crouch and fold until you die. Radio crackling. Slit sparkling. Maybe I liked the fear of being exposed.

'Yara Yavelberg, baby.'

I was breathing too hard. I heard all the men laugh.

Bryan handed me a bunch of twenties when we were done. I counted two hundred bucks. He told me to leave the shoes on the rack and the garment in the bag. Bryan stuck his tongue in my mouth before I went back on the highway. On his pink lingerie, I left a vestige of paste.

✦

Don't get swallowed by the Satanic big three, someone wrote on a Yahoo listserv for porn.

Girls need coke to survive in pornography.

Put the money in your pocket, girls, not up your nose.

Don't get your boobs done by Dr. Sheingold!

The computer at the Starlight was lit by a light bulb crawling with fruit flies. A hard drive in the corner had a handwritten sign. Do not reboot. Do not let your girlfriend tell you you've been body-snatched.

In an email, I learned that Alan had filed my deposition. He advised that I come back to Canada until we heard from Manaus. The timing of receiving a court date or a settlement, he said, would be difficult to assess.

You are safer with us than on your own, Alan wrote. *In America, no less.*

The Yahoo listserv was massive. It had all these posts on Josh Dee.

Josh Dee makes girls' toes curl.

He knows how to talk to pussy.
Dude is in it for the love.
Too bad his brain cells are weak.
Fuck that guy.
Rapist.
Girls give themselves to him.

At the computer in the Starlight, I clicked from Josh Dee to Gilad Shalit. I read that now Egypt was involved in the case. They'd just helped negotiate a deal for thousands of Palestinian prisoners in exchange for Gilad. It was all happening just like Joel had said.

I remember when Gabby told me that Tal was upset in Israel.

Tal was the one who diagnosed my so-called statutory rape.

Someone thought Josh Dee was a rapist.

My daughter misses her sister from the Amazon, Alan wrote.

On another branch of the listserv, it seemed like everyone hated Israel.

Jews want to trick us and own us like slaves.

The Protocols of Zion, someone wrote. *It's been spelled out since then.*

IDF are Nazis.

Jew girls have horns.

I thought they were joking. But I knew they were not.

I stayed up all night zigzagging through Yahoo so I didn't feel alone.

When I finally went back to my motel room, it was almost dawn. I slept and kept the curtains open. I dreamt of my mom.

Return to me, Yara, she said dolefully.

At noon, I drank Diet Coke instead of coffee.

I shaved again, round and round, sawing off sharp little thorns.

I didn't feel static. I had to go on.

✦

PINK TV had a frosted glass door and fancy black cars parked out front in diagonal rows. I thought about my grandmother's sugar cubes in her mint-green sugar pot. She put the cubes between her teeth and drank tea through the sugar like that.

I rang the gold bell. I felt the sun on my head. I wore the same butterfly tank dress and the same sandals, Israeli-made. I thought that my Manson-girl feeling had worked at Naughty Nice. Going one step up, I felt superstitious. But I wasn't into omens. I was into California sun. I thought, true crime has three vectors. *Victim* is first. The second is *detective* who will not give up. *Killer* is the path that I hadn't yet been on.

'Shalom!' Josh Dee said, sticking his head out the door.

He looked left and right. He seemed fake paranoid. I wanted to laugh, but I didn't want him to see me as weak. I didn't expect the star to be right there, answering the door. Josh Dee was the most famous person I'd met in real life. He looked exactly like he did on the oblong phone screen in Israel. Hands around that girl's neck, poofy-haired, extremely white teeth.

Josh Dee ushered me in and locked the door behind us. The ceiling had white-painted pipes. A shag rug on cement.

'You're here for casting, I hope. I bet you know who I am.'

'Yeah,' I said, blushing.

My blushing was a surprise.

'Full name: Joshua Dee. Born in Sacramento.'

'I'm Yara,' I said, smiling.

'Where you from?'

'Israel,' I said. 'Near Ashkelon.'

'Oh, yeah. We're good. Israeli girls know how to fuck.'

Josh bowed dramatically and waved me through another frosted glass door. I had to walk by him. He smelled like Pine-Sol. I could feel his eyes on my ass in the butterfly tank dress. We walked through the centre of an office filled with rows of desks. Josh hummed and waved at people who wore headphones and sat in front of large computer screens. I'd never seen so many computers. Some of them played porn. No one looked at me and Josh Dee. No one waved back at him.

'Right to the back, lady. Follow the sign.'

I opened another frosted door that said STUDIO.

Inside this room, the walls were black and soundproofed. There was a shiny brown couch and a video camera on a tripod. Josh handed me a shiny can with a skull and crossbones.

'For energy,' he said, wiggling his eyebrows exaggeratedly.

I told myself in California that I wouldn't write my girlfriend again. I should've gone for a walk around the Starlight. Anything but talk to her. But it was the feeling of stabbing I wanted. I needed to attack.

Alan had begged me to not engage.

I've been thinking about how we met, I typed. *I've been thinking about it a lot.*

I think about that, too, Yara. I think about it all the time.

Did you care about our age difference?

I'm so happy you are writing. I'm so happy we're talking again.

But for me there was a rent in the fabric. I was on my third Starlight beer.

According to my lawyers, I typed, *you made child porn.*

What are you talking about, typed my girlfriend. *Why do you have LAWYERS, Yara?*

I could feel her blood freeze.

Our fucking is healing, I typed.

'Some of us are lifers,' Josh said. 'Some of us dip in and out.'

There was a long pause in our chat.

I am not ashamed of my feelings like you are, my girlfriend wrote.

Ashamed was not what I was. Ashamed meant nothing in California.

If you tell her details about our case, Alan wrote me, *the case will be ruined.*

I was stabbing in and out of things. That's who I was now.

Manny told me that you're in California.

How the fuck did Manny know where I was?

'Porn is a business and an art,' Josh said. 'I knew from a very young age that this is what I wanted to be.'

You crossed a line, I typed. *I was fifteen years old.*

I knew I was fucking up my position with every message to her.

You saw me as willing, I wrote. *You saw me as ready for you.*

My heart beat triple speed. I was finally stabbing her.

I'd never even kissed someone before. I'd just had a nose job. You came on so strong. I'll never be that vulnerable again.

Good news, Yara. Time to grow up.

I gripped the edge of the desk at the Starlight. I wanted to kill her.

Did I give you the impression I wanted to be pimped out for sex?

Pimped out? Are you deluded? I'm laughing, Jesus Christ.

'I wouldn't shill for PINK TV,' Josh announced, 'if I didn't fully believe in what they do.'

You can't tell me you weren't into it. I will never believe that.

Josh Dee handed me another can of energy drink. His eyes travelled up and down as the fizz infiltrated my blood.

My girlfriend wrote: *I always knew, Yara, that you liked dick.*

'The thing with this industry is that it is hard work but you love it,' Josh said. 'It's a family, Yara. You have to really love having sex.'

My pussy was a cloud dripping condensation.

My mind, on the ground, a puddle of rain.

A man with long white hair in a suit walked through the frosted glass door.

'Beautiful,' he said, looking me up and down. 'Let's get her a test.'

'What do you say, Queen? Energy kicking in?'

The man held out his hand to me. 'I'm Steve Rosenberg.'

It occurred to me Steve had probably been to Israel. He'd been through the hallways of Yad Vashem. He'd eaten sticky pink falafels with his wife and his kids.

After we shook hands, Steve put his hand on my neck.

America is the devil's playground, wrote my girlfriend. *You do not belong there.*

I would never go back to her.

Steve ambled to the camera and adjusted the lens from the front. My heart pumped, copacetic.

'Joshie, give her one of the red slips. She would look great in crimson.'

Josh Dee was like a boxer, jumping around. I thought of Rabbi Fishman dancing, our sweat glands in bloom. Josh Dee took off his T-shirt and then unzipped his jeans. We were going to fool around on camera in front of Steve Rosenberg.

Yara, you're gay. Just come to terms with it. Fuck.

I heard Alan's warning for the last time: *Do not write back to her. Not a word.*

'I love these studio lights,' Josh Dee said. 'Infrared heat.'

Then Josh started slapping his chest and his cock moved like a third mini-fist.

I imagined Steve's stringy white hair in two braids coiled around his head.

'I can tell she's got talent,' Steve said. 'Can we call her Mona?'

'Mona?' Josh laughed. 'Absolutely no way.'

'We let the kids kiss at PINK. We think kissing's okay.'

I never said I was gay. I liked words, I liked names. I was experimental. I liked making meaning.

I light candles, wrote my girlfriend. *I cry for the future of this world.*

My deposition was going to be read by a judge in Manaus.

Josh held the fist in his underpants.

'Sit down now, Yara. We've got the cam on.'

Steve took off his suit jacket, purple silk lined the back. Josh moved his eyebrows and put my hands on his cock.

'The whole point of this, babe, is for people to see how beautiful you are.'

My pussy felt like icing. Icing made of silt. It was so cold I could slide on it like a rink.

'Mmmm, I love that you're nervous, babe. I fucking love nerves about sex.'

I had a long way to go until I was thirty years old.

'Has it been a long time since you've got yourself fucked?'

His cock bulged in my palm. I remembered it made that girl squirt.

'I love her, Steve. I love *Yara*. Let's keep her real name.'

Josh led me to the couch by the heat of his dick. He pulled a cardboard box out from under the couch. Squatted and waved a red piece of silk like a flag.

'I'd give anything, Yara, to see your mouth on my cock.'

Josh held the slip an inch from my face. Josh knows how to talk to pussy. Brain cells dripped out of my head.

'You okay, Queen?' he whispered.

'Take off her shirt for her, Joshie, as part of the tape.'

Josh grabbed my wrists and lifted my arms. He took off my dress.

'Oh yeah, rag doll. I love it,' he said.

'Wow,' Steve whistled. 'Really nice tits.'

I remembered her nipples like thumbprints that day. I remembered how she walked, hip to hip in the wind. I wanted her out of the room. I tried to scrub my mind clean.

'Can you do that from behind and show us how they hang?'

Steve was the director. It should've been Tal.

'I'm gonna touch your breasts now, Yara. Is that okay?'

Josh was behind me. I must've nodded again.

'We like it when they jiggle.'

Josh rubbed the red silk on my breasts. His hands felt so hot. Lingerie, a cum rag. I heard his breath thicken on the uptick. I had to repair everything.

Cold air from the ceiling. My tits covered with silk.

'Lean your head back, Yara. Lean into me now.'

Josh glued my hands on the couch and he slid off my underwear. I felt hungry and thirsty and built like a cow.

'Oh yeah, this is hot.'

My freezing cold cunt. The cum rag on fire. The darkening light.

'I'd like to hang you like a clothespin, baby, right off my fucking dick.'

'Whoa. This is real. She's not acting,' Steve said.

Limp dolls, golem, Daddy: breathe me to life.

Josh put his weight on me from behind. He bit my neck. I liked that. He kept rubbing my tits with the silk. I humped the edge of the couch. I felt our roughly shaved skin. Steve wheeled the camera in. I looked back and snarled. I heard Steve's balloon breaths. Josh moved his hands to my waist.

'Fuck, she's so wet.'

'Keep her bent over like that.'

'She doesn't need the teddy, man. She's doing it all by herself.'

They didn't pay for auditions at PINK TV. My panties disappeared. I remembered myself stuck on my grandmother's couch. My pestle and mortar were fused. We were all photographed.

'I love this. Oh, Yara. Fucking God. Jesus Christ.'

My road to Damascus was the Van Nuys strip mall.

'Can I kiss you?' Josh asked.

'Yeah, kiss me,' I said.

'Did she sign a release?'

'Sorry, man, Steve. She just wanted to start.'

Josh stuck his tongue in my mouth. I was the messenger of sex.

Tal and Rabbi Fishman were my interlocuters.

I thought, golem, go get 'em. I have a soul inside me.

'You have one fucking job, Josh.'

'Fuck. Sorry, man, Steve.'

Steve left the room in a blur. Then Josh pushed his cock in my cunt. I grunted. It hurt.

'You are very naughty, Yara. I'm in big twouble now.'

He pushed in and pulled out. We had sex to make sparks. I heard myself breathing.

'Fuck me,' I said.

I'd never said that before.

'Oh my God, bitch. What are you doing to me?'

Josh fucked. I held on. He skewered and dug. I felt like a balloon being pumped up as big as the sky.

'Yara, hot damn, you are eating my dick.'

Dick was bunk. So was *bitch*. I could change the world with my thoughts. I was a rag doll alive with the stitches undone. My head hung, clothespins gone, I was sucking in souls. Every time he slid in, I was sucking in more. I felt it. I loved it. My tongue touched the couch.

'Joshua, stop it,' Steve yelled, walking back into the room.

My head was so bubbly. Josh rolled it around. Prickly ridges, split seams, a surging long burn.

'Cut it out,' Steve yelled.

I cut her out of my mind.

'Lawsuit, Joshua. The girl hasn't signed.'

'Mommy,' Josh whined.

I started breathing like a dog. Somehow, I was on the floor. I mean, I was on the ground without panties and I couldn't stand up.

'This girl knows how to fuck, Steve. I couldn't resist. We can do oral now. That's not a problem, is it?'

Josh picked me up from the ground. My legs rotated out like a frog's.

'God, she's like honey.'

I signed my name on Steve's wobbling clipboard. Then I fell on the couch. Josh was hard the whole time. He suctioned his mouth like a plug onto my cunt. I felt totally drugged. California was life. I was a girl being fucked in the earth. His tongue was my cunt. I massaged his whole face. Josh kept nodding and slurping me, wraparound, ruler-sized.

And my girlfriend was banished. She was not a part of this land. Skull and crossbones, a periscope cunt. Steve was somehow perched over me, holding my chin.

'I don't normally do this,' Steve said. 'I have a great wife.'

Steve held his cock through his pants. Cocks were like pine cones, I thought. Bumped and deformed. Maybe my girlfriend was right. This was the Devil's playground. The tape was still running. I felt split in half. Josh made my clit huge. He was painting his face with my cunt. *Dick* should be *pine cone*, I thought. *Pussy* means love.

The vines on Tal's house were curlicue, black. Steve fondled my breasts. Josh kept swivelling his head. His forehead pulsed on my belly. His slurring tongue inside me. I'm not gay, I'm not straight. I'm an alien. God. I squirted inside him. I let him drink me.

'Fuck yeah, my Yara. Queen of honey.'

My lips were all slurry, producing vernix. A cold wet spot on the couch, an excruciating itch.

'Steve, man, she's burning. Can you get this onscreen?'

Steve-man was limping. I guess they fucked girls together all the time. I knew the Blessing of the Heretic from Rabbi Fishman: *May there be no hope for heretics. May You blot out all Your enemies …*

'She looks a little dark, Josh. Make her happy,' Steve said.

Josh pushed away from the floor. He left me open and soaked.

'I'm so fucking hard for you, Yara. I'm gonna stay hard my whole life.'

Then Josh jumped up from the floor and slung his arm around my shoulder on the couch. I didn't want to think of the stuff that was written on Yahoo, like *rapist*. I preferred *cunnilingus* to *squirt*. Then Josh was beside me on the couch and it was like we were watching TV. I leaned into his underarm and smiled at Steve. Me and Josh started to kiss like Rabbi Fishman and his wife.

'Lemme see her big teeth.'

I thought of gouge marks in buildings. Tunnels dug. Tal's grassy backyard filled with deer.

'Ask her, Josh, if she'll do Black, DP.'

'Please, my princess baby doll, marry me.'

Yara, wrote my girlfriend, *you abandoned me*.

The factory softened. Its walls curved in. I felt drugged, I felt conscious. I felt holy.

✦

We know where you are. We see your IP *address.*

She wants to come and get you, Manny messaged. *When she read that lawyer's paper, I've never seen her like that.*

I knew they couldn't find me by an IP address. Maybe they knew I was in California, maybe even Van Nuys. But they didn't know that I was moving in with Josh and shooting real pornography.

She can't stop crying, Manny wrote. *She said she's going to kill herself.*

Josh Dee had a spare room in his condominium. The baby's room, he called it, filled up with books. Josh showed me his collection of California pulp, shelves of paperbacks, alphabetized and wrapped in plastic sleeves. *Trollop Trade.*

Street Lover. Fifty Dollars a Night. A young actress 'who co-operated fully in the corruption of her own innocence.'

I loved the way the books looked. They reminded me of my true crime. I took a book called *Ball Me Again* from the shelf. A girl bit another girl's shoulder on the cover.

I thought you loved her, Manny wrote.

'There was a time, Yara, when things were easy in the industry,' Josh said. 'You snorted a couple of lines and made thousands a night. But the Golden Age ended in '98 or '99. You know, when bitches started spitting in each other's mouths, that kind of thing.'

Josh took *Ball Me Again* from my hands and shelved it back in place.

'They want to burn the archives. Anti-porn people fucking love to burn things.'

Josh had moved me out of the motel and into his king-sized bed. I now had multiple pillows of feathers under my head. He said he wanted to keep me legal in the U.S. Josh told me he had lawyers. His parents lived in Ventura. His father, he said, was a celebrity cardiologist.

'So, would I feel shame, Yara, if I was a gynecologist? My parents are proud of what I have accomplished. They support me fully.'

Josh didn't know that I had a lawyer. He didn't know anything about me.

'What are you doing in California?' my mother had asked me on the phone.

'I have a theatre job.'

'What theatre? Can I come visit and see you onstage?'

So far in California, I felt weighed down and hungry and tired a lot. The Starlight had a pay phone in the parking lot.

'I just want you to be happy,' my mother sighed.

I knew it was too quick to move in with Josh Dee.

You lie to me, wrote my girlfriend. *You've lied about everything.*

I hadn't ever considered moving in with her. It was like she knew what I was doing. But she wouldn't let me loose.

'Yara,' my mother said. 'I want you to be out in the world.'

I used to love her, I said to Manny. *I loved her truly.*

Out as gay. Out as porn star. Out as scapegoat.

✦

Their house was a palace, something kings lived in. Marble floors, spiral staircase, everything stainless-steel, mirror clean.

Josh's mother was short with an oversized head and large nose. She looked like a mouse, holding her arms, nibbling in the vestibule.

'I'm Gillian, that's Art,' she said. 'Joshie's told us all about you.'

'I like Israeli girls from the military.' Art winked at me.

He was shorter than Josh, with black stubble, white hair.

'Beautiful country,' Gillian gushed. 'Gorgeous people. Vegetarian.'

'Guys, you're embarrassing her,' Josh said, wrapping his arm around me.

Their kitchen was the same size as my girlfriend's whole place. There were sliding glass doors and an outdoor dinner table already set. The backyard seemed to sit on a cliff, over-looking other palaces.

'What does your family do, Yara?'

'Uh, my mother is a paralegal,' I said. 'My grandmother's from Ashkelon ...'

'Yara wants to stay in California,' Josh announced.

Josh poured me something yellow and fizzy in a flute.

'I need to talk to Dad,' Josh said, winking at me and his mom.

'Let's let the boys grill,' she said. 'Come for a tour.'

I put down the drink that Josh gave me. Gillian looped her arm possessively through mine.

'Do you like it here?' she asked as she led me through a gold-striped hallway.

I would never have known this woman was over fifty years old. Maybe she'd had a face lift, or a boob job. I touched their gold wallpaper. It felt like sand. We walked up the curved marble staircase with Gillian stuck to my side. I had on a thick-strapped black sundress that Josh had vetted. He said that his parents were cool, but to be modest, not crass.

'Yara, finding a good man is important in life.'

We were climbing the staircase really slowly. Gillian cooed.

'I know you're a very young woman, but it helps to think ahead.'

Upstairs, one long hallway led to so many doors. We wove in and out of all the bedrooms with TVs nailed to the walls.

'This is where my oldest studied for the LSATs. This is where my youngest daughter cried. She is married now, thank God, but she's making me wait for babies.'

We stopped in a room filled with books at the end of the hallway.

'This is where our Joshua used to live. He had a lot of girls up here all through high school,' Gillian said. 'My middle boy was always into sex. Yara, I think I can be frank.'

High school Josh had a king-sized bed with a studded leather headboard.

'At one point we took him to a psychologist, but nothing really changed with all the doctors, or with the meds. Eventually, we had to accept our kid was fine just as he is. Josh says that the industry uses every skill he has.'

Gillian smiled, staring at me. Josh had her brainwashed, I thought. Or maybe porn was as good as gynecology. But I knew my mother wouldn't buy that.

'Still, we've always been a bit worried, Yara, that he won't settle down. He's thirty years old now. It's getting to be time for that.'

Gillian stroked my arm up and down. Did she know that her son had said 'marry me' when we fucked?

'Are you okay, Yara? You're a wisp of thing. You look like you arrived here from outer space.'

'Israel,' I said.

Gillian nodded. 'Am Yisrael Chai.'

'May I use the bathroom?'

'I can't vouch for its cleanliness.'

I unstuck myself from her. I headed to Joshua's private high school bathroom. Black tubs of protein powders and bags of Epsom salts were jammed under the sink. Did my grandmother want me to find a rich husband like this? My grandmother wore opal rings on every finger and danced with her friends. I remembered her throwing out the Israeli records that she loved because Shlomo Carlebach was accused by his followers of rape.

I had pins and needles in my legs. Rape was following me around.

I bet Gillian wanted Josh to be married in Israel.

When I went back downstairs, they were all sitting outside. Tea lights punctured the backyard. The sky seemed starless.

'These taste like the real thing,' Art said, licking his thumb.

'We eat a lot of fermented products in this family,' Gillian said, handing me a burger bun.

I sat down at the table. Josh squeezed my thigh.

He was the same age as my girlfriend. He was a burger flipper, too. He wanted to devour me. Flatten me. I recognized that now.

Become more fucking solid, I thought, or get swallowed again.

How could I become more solid? Feed all my dark needs.

✦

Me and my girlfriend went to Mindu for our fourth anniversary with a picnic on our backs. I had been talking to her about what I should do with my life. I thought I wanted to go to São Paulo. I wanted to go to university. At almost nineteen, I spent full days on her couch all day reading. I was reading Stephen King and my true crime like an addict. But also, everything by José Saramago and the American poet H.D. I was thinking about studying English. I could translate English books to Portuguese. This was a vague thought but it occupied me.

My girlfriend told me that I should write my own book.

'I work hard,' she said. 'I work hard for our food. You can stay home and write all day if you want.'

She said that love takes one person who is completely full-time.

My girlfriend baked us cake and packed us sandwiches and fruit. She said the preparations took her half the night. I had no interest in homemaking. She told me she hadn't slept. I'd slept at home that night because my mom wanted me to meet her new boyfriend. My mom let this guy smoke indoors. We'll get rid of the smell later, she said to me with a smile. She served me and her boyfriend steak and paletas and wine. Her boyfriend sucked so hard on his cigarettes that the paper wrinkled like a skirt. He smiled at me and said, Your mom is so nice.

I'd recently read the book that Stephen King wrote about learning how to write. He said that you had to connect to your character's soul. I thought a lot about that. Where was my soul? Where was hers? If you changed your face, was the soul altered as well? Stephen King made me think about murder and writing and rescuing souls. I thought, writing is where you discovered someone.

At Mindu, as we ate, my girlfriend got on one knee even though we were both sitting down. We were at our armless green bench, the place where we'd first kissed.

'You are the only one for me in this life,' she said.

Then my girlfriend took out a gold ring, a band with a malachite stone.

My sandwich had a bite in it, lodged without form.

Soul was something I really did not understand. *Soul* felt elusive, like a speck, not in a body or mind.

My girlfriend said that this ring had been blessed.

'Yara, I want you to be my wife,' she said. Her voice cracked.

I immediately knew that I didn't want to get married to her. But I had to take the ring. There was no in-between place where I could say no.

My girlfriend's eyes swelled. 'Every day, every hour, I love you a little bit more.'

I thought of the equator, of days that did not turn into night.

'Thank you,' I said, before she wedged it over my knuckle like a noose.

My girlfriend sprung off her knee and kissed me on the tip of my nose.

'Oh my God,' she said. 'It looks so beautiful on you.'

She held my ringed hand like she'd never touched it before. I felt like this wasn't real. How was I going to tell her to wait? I'd talked to my girlfriend about travelling all the time. She knew how much I wanted to see New York and Paris, the islands of Greece. My girlfriend said once when she was drunk that life was a simulation. I thought her eyes were dead then, and mine were, too. Like their purpose had been suctioned. It would be better to not see. Maybe this was a dream. Maybe the ring was not real. I felt something – my soul? – squirting helter-skelter.

'You like it?' my girlfriend asked, wiping her tears.

'I like it,' I said.

A group of guys were walking down the path toward our spot. No one ever came here by this bench. I didn't want to look.

'You're not acting like you like it.'

'I love you. Thank you.'

I just needed one moment with my girlfriend where nothing went wrong. I hugged her, hooking my chin over her arm. My guts started to roil. I knew the guys coming closer to us from my high school.

'Hey, it's Yara Yavelberg!'

They were almost at our bench. We weren't hugging anymore.

'Tell them to go,' she said. 'Leave us alone.'

I started to shiver. My girlfriend kissed me. That was the worst thing to do. I heard the guys' laughter like liquid sloshing. I didn't want to kiss. I'd never imagined being proposed to like this.

'Yara, girl. It's been a while.'

'Hey,' I said, peeling away from my girlfriend.

The food on the blanket in front of us looked green. There was a beetle at my sandwich. My girlfriend stood up and reached for my hand.

But I wanted to stay on the bench, all tied up. I could feel her getting mad.

'Don't you want to introduce us to your friend?'

I shook my head no.

'Show them your ring,' my girlfriend said.

The three guys started laughing, ocean sloshing echoes again.

'You never told us you were a lesbian, Yara.'

'Baby, please stand up.'

My girlfriend yanked me up from the bench and held me so tight. She put her hands on my ass. It was like I was numb. These guys weren't my friends. They were laughing at us. Then my girlfriend left me and I saw her punch one of them right in the stomach. One guy stepped on our food and one knocked over the wine. Red bled into the grass. The malachite on my finger itched like a wart.

'I'll kill your mothers!' yelled my girlfriend.

The guys started to laugh. My girlfriend was crying, she said she was calling Manny. She rooted around in her backpack for her cellphone.

The three guys walked away and they didn't look back.

I thought, if you marry your girlfriend, your whole life will be like this. It will be crisis to crisis, clothespin for a brain. No school, no translation, no soul to be found.

Josh took me to the observatory on the side of Mount Hollywood.

'When we're married, Yara,' he said, 'we'll schedule all our time. You work, then I'll work, so things are equal with us. I'll take care of our babies. I'll be a good dad.'

He rubbed my arm like his mother as we walked through the museum.

'Being pregnant, it's gonna be awesome. I wuv pregnant goddesses.'

Josh already tired me out. I had no desire for that. He spoke like a baby often. I was not ready to be pregnant. I saw Gabby sobbing on the tablecloth, my mother pitching cigarettes downstream. I saw Sharon Tate, mother-to-be, eviscerated by actresses.

'I don't want to have children yet,' I said. 'Obviously.'

'But the second you see our kid, you're gonna love it so much. Girls like you, Yara, are programmed to procreate.'

He was talking about my breasts. The way that he looked at me, I felt like he could fuck me on the floor in front of all these schoolkids.

I associated motherhood with mayhem and my grandmother's photographs of dead girls.

The Griffith Observatory was gold-domed, massive.

'Don't worry, baby, you'll get there.' Josh winked. 'I'm thirty now. It's time to make little Joshies and Yaras in the tub.'

'Daddy, I don't want babies,' I said, baby-talking, making a joke.

'Don't call me that,' Josh said, leading to the refracting telescope.

I wanted to see Saturn.

'I take every girl here after we've had sex.'

Josh had no filter. He only had a dick.

At Griffith Observatory, through the biggest telescope, I saw no fireworks.

Josh Dee was just like my girlfriend, bombing me with love.

'You're not from Israel, Yara, are you?' Josh said. 'Tell me the truth.'

Through the lens, I saw nothing. The hole was totally flat.

'Just don't lie to my mother. She can tell when you're lying,' Josh said.

I wanted to call my mother a lot. I started calling her every day.

She said, You can come home, Yara, as long as you're not going back to her.

My mother made me feel that my mistakes had all been magnified.

I should've seen stars through the telescope. I should've seen something.

✦

After we had been living together for a few weeks, Josh woke me up in the middle of the night. He said he liked it when I was confused.

He said, 'When we have kids, it's not gonna be the same. Yara, we gotta take advantage of everything now.'

I did not ever give my girlfriend's ring back. It sat in one of my mom's old ashtrays, in pasted-down ash.

I knew that Josh Dee didn't want to feel like I was smarter than him. We had a ten-year age difference. I felt stuck on repeat.

'I'm telling you, Yara, I'm a beast around you.'

My guilt was molten, like gold being poured into bricks. I knew that multiple lawyers had now read all our chats from Israel. Multiple lawyers had seen the video that Manny sent when I was sixteen years old. Yes, I was guilty of leaving her when she was distressed. Yes, I was guilty of stealing her malachite ring. But I didn't want a court case. I wanted to forget.

I'd thought that my life would be mine, finally, in California. But Josh woke me up to fuck me in my sleep.

Maybe I regretted my nose job. Maybe I regretted Mindu Park. But I didn't want to be here. I wanted my mom.

Josh led me to the bathroom, holding me up by the armpits. I arose from the tomb of unconsciousness. Air conditioning, ice water, sticky dead flesh. Did Fishman from Philadelphia know about porn's telescope? Did anyone know about it but me?

The floor in Josh's adult bathroom was raised pink and pockmarked. I really didn't know why the sink was filled up with ice cubes.

'Are you awake, babe? Yes or no. Easy Q, Queen.'

Josh held me by the neck as we looked in the mirror. We were like rabbit and butcher, a simulation, his dark needs.

'Wakey-wakey, wifey.'

Josh's smile was fake. His helmet head, too. Why did I let myself fall asleep in his bed?

'Let me go lie down,' I said, with a bunny-rabbit twitch.

Josh lifted up my arms. He'd bought me some crimson slip thing. It was a camisole and panties with a slit that looked like gym shorts.

'Top off,' Josh said, tracing a line down my spine.

What fucking story did I walk right into? I saw myself in Israel. I saw myself in Toronto. Tal would not let this happen to her. God, what did I do wrong?

Unconsciousness is a space of deep healing, my girlfriend said. In Umbanda, it's the mother, not the father, who rules everything.

There was a mirror in front of me. A sink filled with ice.

Josh had very flat eyes and one hand on my neck.

I had to figure this out before the murderer was murdered, I thought.

We live in a world, said my girlfriend, that is totally upside down.

I prayed to the abyss: escape this true crime. I was panicked.

Suddenly, I was back in the clinic, strapped to the surgical chair. Women pulled down and pulled up their tube tops for doctors.

I just had my nose broken. I felt pain like a worm does: cut her and slice her and she'll flatten to adapt.

I thought, memory was weird with a mushy bottom.

Josh pulled my silk shorts to the side and wiggled his knuckle in. He said that a woman should have a baby before she is twenty-five.

I almost didn't feel his finger. I wanted goose feathers in bed. I had five years to understand this.

I had a premonition. Death was going to come.

This condo was a crypt. California, the crossroads.

Then Josh pushed my whole head into a sink full of ice.

I was thinking under there. I thought, he is going to lift me up. Why did he want me to drown? Do not understand. Ice cubes banged my cheekbones like loose, washed-up teeth.

I realized he'd locked my wrists with one hand. A wrestler does this, I thought. I was still thinking logically. I'd never thought sex was close to death.

My girl had loved me and I'd loved her back.

Statutory rape, I heard in Tal's voice.

No brain cells. No safe words. I had to get out of this scene. Josh Dee had his ring finger locked inside of me.

Most girls at PINK TV think Josh is a little kooky, Steve said.

Steve winked at me when I signed the contract.

They just love what I'm serving, Josh added, wiggling his hips.

I would not accept that all my mistakes led me to this.

Josh finally pulled me up and cranked me to him by the jaw. He stuck his tongue in my mouth. My skull felt air-conditioned.

My girlfriend would never have hurt me on purpose. We were just differently wired. She didn't want me to expire.

'Even when they tell me to stop,' Josh said, 'I know they don't want me to.'

I heard myself gulp like a fish in the frigid bathroom. This was what the man wanted: my limp-doll panic. I just needed a second. I would get all my thoughts back.

'Stop,' I said.

Josh Dee shoved me back under the ice. He did the same stroke down my back as he did inside.

Gillian, you raised a sociopath, bitch.

You don't want to get married to Josh? she'd asked me in his teenage bedroom.

I don't want to die in your son's condominium!

I do not want to be packed in his heifer-sized, stainless-steel fridge. Even Gabby and Alan do not have a deluxe box like that. Josh stacked his refrigerator with energy drinks. Every single day, he went through a dozen cans. He lifted me again out of the sink by my hair.

'Stop,' I said. 'Red.'

'Once we have kids, I'll stop waking you up.'

He dunked me back under. This time was clearer, like ice. I remembered my girlfriend had a freezer that always broke down. She wanted my soul to be softer and braided with hers. I thought of my mother, my grandmother, her mother, my mother's mothers being stunted in the world. I blew a final bubble. Josh's fingers went blue. I'll solve this, I thought. Crack the riddle right here.

✦

In Itacoatiara, that night after our visit to her family, my girl-friend was sick all over the floor of the guesthouse bathroom. I didn't leave her. I cleaned up. I gave her a bath. She kept apologizing to me and I kept telling her it was okay. When we fell asleep, I wrapped myself around her back. We stayed in the room the entire next day. I got her plantains and fried fish from a street vendor near the beach. Later, we had sex. The birds near our window sounded like mice. I wanted to go to the ocean and feel the hot sand on my back. But I stayed in that room with her, as shitty as it was. When we kissed, when we fucked, I heard the birds in my head. Her mouth was like syrup. Her tongue, candy cane.

'I'm sorry, Yara. This is my fault. You don't deserve this.'

My girlfriend put her whole self inside me. I deserved everything.

♦

A skinny girl with brown skin bounced around in the pool.

'Yara, meet Little Mina, our hottest new girl.'

'Fuck you, Josh Dee,' Little Mina screamed. 'I've been here a year!'

Little Mina's bikini was coiled on the deck. Men stood around the perimeter, smoking and staring.

A fluorescent wave rippled on Little Mina's pyramid nose. Her black hair hung in a braid under a white baseball cap.

'Mina's Arab,' Josh said. 'I mean, Muslim. Same thing, am I right?'

'Hey.' Little Mina smiled at me. 'Ignore this numbskull. I have an extra bathing suit in the basement. We look about the same size. We should go rock climbing together, what do you think?'

I thought, two scapegoats scaling the side of a cliff. I was still shivering from last night, my head in the sink.

I sat down cross-legged on the deck. I really felt dizzy, unclear. I'd called Tal crying. Little Mina made fluorescent blue spirals in the shallow end with her nails.

'I don't usually do girl-on-girl,' she said to me, 'but Rosenberg showed me your tape. That looked like an exorcism, girl! I thought, okay, gimme some of that.'

I couldn't smile. Little Mina hoisted herself out of the pool. She was naked. I stared.

'Give me a towel, you Neanderthals!' she screamed.

Some guy wrapped her shoulders with a cape. Little Mina didn't take off her baseball cap.

'Let's go,' she said.

'Go on,' Josh said to me.

He pinched Little Mina's ass. She swatted him away.

We walked through sliding glass doors of the house past some older women in the kitchen, cooking us lunch. It smelled like onions and beef.

'Change room's in the basement.'

Little Mina found her purse on the floor. It was shiny white, with gold buckles, pillowed like my grandmother's headboard. Little Mina waved at the women in the kitchen and led me down the stairs. She had puppet legs, skinny and jointed, big hips. In the basement, the floor was marbled. Little Mina's lips had turned blue.

'You like to smoke, Yara? You new to all this?'

I didn't know what to say or how to say it as she dug in her purse. I felt whipped back to zero. I felt silent again. I had to remember myself. I had to get myself back. Tal was coming to California to see me.

'You don't have to stay with Josh Dee, you know. Everyone seems to start there. He acts like God's gift to females. It's all a fucking lie. Come sit with me. Over here. Closer, Yara.'

Little Mina extracted a joint, perfectly pinched at the end. I felt my tongue stirring. I wanted to cry.

'I do this for cash. Sometimes it's fun. This shit's from my boyfriend. Jamaica. Direct.'

Little Mina lit the spliff. I still felt the ice in my teeth.

'You can do this for a while and then you move on.'

We were passing her boyfriend's joint back and forth. I started to feel the smoke loosening me.

'I love your nose, babe. Where'd you get it done?'

'My mother got it for me when I was fifteen,' I said.

'Forward fucking thinking, Mama! I wish my mother thought I was hot.'

I laughed.

'I'm serious,' Little Mina said. 'My mother said I was part troglodyte.'

I took the joint from her again. 'You're beautiful,' I said.

'You want to stay at my place tonight? My Jamaican's away.'

I had signed a contract for one thousand dollars for this.

'Don't be stressed,' Little Mina said. 'We'll just finish this up. Josh Dee can go fuck himself. Forget about him.'

Upstairs in the sun, I lay on my back on the deck. Little Mina, a goddess, slid my bikini bottoms off. She used her tongue, stuck it in. I could not relax.

I had no peripheral vision. All I smelled was chlorine. I wriggled with Little Mina to obliteration.

I didn't need sex with my head in a sink.

✦

Tal rented us a hotel room on Hollywood Boulevard. Cotton white sheets on a king-sized bed with a white leather headboard. Josh had been calling me on repeat. I'd gotten a little cellphone, a red flip.

Tal unpacked her big camera and her notebook on the fluffy bedspread. She had her father's recorder, a bunch of miniature tapes.

Tal looked at me. 'I know my script was shit.'

When I stayed the night with Little Mina, we drank tequila and got really stoned. We watched grainy Russian porn on her boyfriend's desktop.

A lot of girls are sober now, Little Mina said. But girls become sober for a reason, correct?

Me and Tal ordered tacos. We got room-service beers.

'Look, Yara, I don't believe that porn can ever be, I don't know, significant.'

We ate from Styrofoam on the bedspread. I guzzled my beer.

'The only problem with porn is dissociation,' I said.

'What do you mean?'

'It means you leave your body – which is a skill.'

'Are you okay if we tape this conversation?' Tal asked. 'Because I think what you're talking about has ramifications. I mean, for other people, other places, for the freedom of girls.'

I felt like the word *freedom* was hyperbolic.

'You need to speak more, Yara,' Tal said. 'You have things to say.'

Me and Little Mina had seen girls onscreen leaving themselves. We actually saw it, I mean. Girls floating out of themselves. We laughed so hard. A mutual hallucination.

'I think being a "teen slut" highlights a double, in-and-out body stand,' I said. 'Like, you have this feeling of being pumped full of life and then total numbness.'

Me and Little Mina had watched this one porn where a guy was masturbating with a girl's feet. She was on her stomach, staring at the wrinkled pillow. There was a magazine on the night table and a transistor radio in her hands. She was fiddling with the tuning, in control of the scene.

'Outward distractions signify the inward,' I told Tal. 'In porn, there's female schism and that schism is a feat. Like, a girl can be two places at once. She becomes omnipotent.'

'That's … I don't know,' Tal said. 'I mean, I've never seen that.'

Maybe she didn't feel things or see things like me and Little Miya did. Tal hadn't just escaped death in an embalming condominium.

'It's a porn trope,' I said. 'I mean, being mute. A girl onscreen is acting, on her belly, crossed ankles kicking the air. She doesn't want to talk. You think she wants to be alone. But her toes keep fake-accidentally touching the big coiled dick behind her. She's facing away, eyes on something else. She's not looking at the guy's penis, all his energy, bulging out of his shorts.'

'I hate the word *dick*,' Tal said.

'Me, too. I call them pine cones.'

'So, in this porn, when the girl finally spoke, she just said: "What are you doing?" "Nothing," the guy replied. So, then the girl just went back to just zoning out, coy.'

'Zoning out, coy,' Tal repeated, trying to understand.

'The guy pushed his penis into the cervix-like gap of her feet.'

Tal wrote notes, her brow furrowed. It was in Russian, that porn. But I had the power of translation.

'So, the girl was still pretending that she didn't know what was going on when of course she did. And when she turned around again, she gave the guy this look of disgust while he was slipping his cock fast in and out of her glued-together, serpentine arch.'

'So, it's comedy?' Tal asked.

'Sometimes,' I said. 'Sometimes it's freakiness. Sometimes it's pleasure. Or fear.'

'Sometimes it's the hatred of women.'

'Sometimes it's a combination.'

I remembered that Little Mina said: Girls get sober when they're ready to feel.

'But men watching porn is different than women, don't you think?' Tal asked.

'Yeah. Men always see things that they want to topple or get in. Women, subject or object, seem to want to mess with the pipes.'

I didn't want to be scared that people were coming after me. I meant my girlfriend and her incarnation Josh Dee.

I said, 'I think what it all comes down to is this: porn works when you – the girl – don't know if you're inside the film or outside.'

✦

The next morning, my phone woke me up in our fancy Hollywood hotel.

'One thousand for a threesome – you, Josh, and Mina,' Steve Rosenberg said.

'Don't go,' Tal said. 'We have things to do.'

Me and Tal had stayed up most of the night. Josh Dee had called on repeat. I didn't answer the phone once. The windows weren't open. The room smelled like cold cream. We said we'd order breakfast from room service and keep recording.

'Can we publish her name?' Tal said.

'I don't want to ruin her life.'

'Consequences are inevitable. She knows that, Jesus Christ.'

'I don't believe I'm completely innocent.'

'C'mon, Yara, that's beside the point.'

'Some people have sex when they are young and some don't.'

'Sex is the most complicated human story that exists for the law.'

Tal had pages of notes from last night. She put in a new tape. I feel like she'd heard this story before. Everyone had. I was storytelling backwards, up my ancestral line.

'Yara, I know my dad is upset that you stopped the process. But I don't feel that way. I understand.'

My legs, pins and needles stabbing in the cotton sheets. We'd talked about porn. I took a deep breath.

'I was changed when I got a nose job at fifteen years old. My girlfriend assisted the doctor.'

I found I could finally listen to myself.

'She wore blue plastic gloves, a face shield, and a mask. She steadied my arm while I went under. My face got mashed into her breasts.

'They broke my nose with a hammer.

'Then they shaved off my bone.

'I felt like Jesus Christ when I woke.'

My grin was a rictus. It had been videotaped.

'My girlfriend told me that I couldn't eat for twenty-four hours. She said I would be sore. I was all wrapped in bandages and bruised, but she said I was beautiful.'

I wanted to knife through the smile of my face.

'She told me that the future would be different, that's what the future means. I would become a whole new woman. I would not always be in pain.

'My girlfriend said, "The future is something that we can create."

'I remember my whole face was hot, as if it was stripped of its skin.

'I remember when she called me the first time I wrapped the phone cord around my finger so tightly that I cut off my circulation – '

Tal interrupted, 'What phone was that?'

'My girlfriend said, "Every person should be worshipped."'

'You were still at the clinic? Hang on, Yara.'

I felt like I was in my own future in that Hollywood room.

'Being worshipped is private,' I said. 'But you can make it public.'

Tal slid the recorder toward me on our bedspread.

'Early on, I remember, she put her hand on my stomach.

'I remember she pushed low down in my gut.

'My girlfriend said, "I think this helps wake people up."

'She made a fist and I remember she started rotating it down. Her fist went in a spiral, like she was digging something out. It felt painful at first, like I had gas. I thought I was going to cry or yell *stop*, but eventually my whole body relaxed.

'"Look at me," she said. "Keep your eyes open now."

'"You look like a painting," she said. "Like your face has been flayed."

'"The channel is almost connected," she said.'

'What channel?' Tal interrupted. She put her hand on my arm. 'Yara, this is weird.'

Tal held her breath. I continued to the end.

'I let her take over the channel because she made it feel good …

'Look, I know it isn't always easy to see how things went with us. I mean, from my nose job to Mindu to my knowledge of sex. I felt so special. She loved me as an actress.'

Tal kept her hand on my arm. The tape kept on taping.

'She said that the reason she chose me out of every other girl was because my channel connected. It worked first on me.'

Tal squeezed my arm. Her palm was so hot. I thought of Little Mina out hustling on set.

My girlfriend would've hated me describing her as a predator like this.

And maybe even more, my words being transcribed.

Two weeks in California had turned into a month.

Tal promised me she'd finish what her father had not.

'Words,' Tal pronounced, 'are mightier than the law.'

I cannot believe, my girlfriend telegraphed, *that you are a porn star.*

The *channel connected* had led me to it. Sometimes it was light-filled, sometimes packed with darkness.

'If you're comfortable with it,' Tal said gently, 'I'd like to use a few stills from the sex tape. I'll blur you, but I think it's important for women to see what it looked like.'

'You should be a lawyer,' I said.

'You should name her,' Tal snapped.

I still felt the fear of my girlfriend's anger.

'It doesn't matter if you loved her. She could do the same thing again.'

'But what if I'm prolonging this by giving it new life?'

'Stop blaming yourself, Yara. This was abuse.'

I thought of my mother on our balcony, leaning against the ledge. The hairy palm tree in our yard hemmed in by a gate. Our circular driveway shone like a half moon. That telescope showed me nothing. I had to detatch from abuse. I knew there was something else wondrous out there in the world. Planets like boils, big blue breasts, throbbing bodies not mine …

'Okay,' I said. 'You can use her real name.'

Tal looked surprised.

'And you can call it abuse. She works at a clinic called Bioplastics.'

Tal smiled at me with her mother's sad face.

'Gloria. Not a predator,' I said.

'I'm sorry, Yara. That's not up to you to declare.'

I stayed for a while at Little Mina's in California with my grandmother's support. I had a plan to end up in New York.

My mother told me she'd visit me wherever I was safe. I think all mothers want their daughters to believe in fairy tales – as if princesses are the opposite of the *Helter Skelter* girls.

I learned that Gilad Shalit was exchanged for 1,027 men and Josh Dee was accused by two women of rape.

Tal published her essay: 'Troubling the Subject in Internet Porn.'

I made money with Little Mina, slithering in pools and on decks. I was going to study translation and true crime.

I stayed in my body. I learned to say *victim* out loud.

Gloria was fired from the clinic. I heard from her only once more.

I suspect one day, Yara, you'll understand what you lost.

But porn was the crook where I found my soul, bloodied and live.

Tamara Faith Berger is the author of *Maidenhead* (2012), *Little Cat* (2013), *Kuntalini* (2016), and *Queen Solomon* (2018). She lives and works in Toronto.

Thank you immeasurably to my editor, Alana Wilcox, and to Crystal Sikma, James Lindsay, and everyone at Coach House Books, as well as to Emily Cook and Natalie Stamatopolous at Cursor, and to Stuart Ross and Ingrid Paulson. Thank you to Lise Soskolne, Tess Chakkalakal, Rachel Fulford, Rosa Pagano, and Rebekah Rutkoff for talking to me about the book. Thanks to Clement, to Wolf, to my parents and sisters for your love.

Typeset in Albertina and ITC Avant Garde Gothic Pro.

Printed at the Coach House on bpNichol Lane in Toronto, Ontario, on
Zephyr Antique Laid paper, which was manufactured, acid-free, in
Saint-Jérôme, Quebec, from second-growth forests. This book was
printed with vegetable-based ink on a 1973 Heidelberg KORD offset litho
press. Its pages were folded on a Baumfolder, gathered by hand, bound
on a Sulby Auto-Minabinda, and trimmed on a Polar single-knife cutter.

Coach House is on the traditional territory of many nations, including
the Mississaugas of the Credit, the Anishnabeg, the Chippewa, the
Haudenosaunee, and the Wendat peoples, and is now home to many
diverse First Nations, Inuit, and Métis peoples. We acknowledge that
Toronto is covered by Treaty 13 with the Mississaugas of the Credit. We
are grateful to live and work on this land.

Edited by Alana Wilcox
Cover design by Ingrid Paulson, cover photos ©iStockPhoto, cover art
    The Scapegoat (1854–55) by William Holman Hunt, National Museums
    Liverpool
Interior design by Crystal Sikma
Author photo by Bradley Golding

Coach House Books
80 bpNichol Lane
Toronto ON M5S 3J4
Canada

416 979 2217
800 367 6360

mail@chbooks.com
www.chbooks.com